"Do all men fall at your feet, Harmony Cross?"

"Maybe I was wrong. Maybe you haven't changed."

He smiled a little, and she saw the lurking sadness again.

"Oh, I think we've both changed." He swung the back of the trailer open. "And I'm sorry for baiting you that way. Old habits and all."

"You're right. Maybe we should call a truce?"

A truce would mean, what? Being friends? The idea felt a little bit dangerous.

"I'm not sure exactly why we need a truce," Dylan said as he stepped up into the trailer and reached for the horse's tail. "Come on, Beau, head on out of there."

Dylan closed the back of the trailer and then the gate. "You understand you can't ride him."

"You understand that I'm very aware of what I can and can't do."

"Why are you so defensive?" he countered.

"Because I'm here to get away from people who feel I need to be told at every turn what I can and can't do."

"So what you're saying is, you've had all of the advice you can handle for a lifetime?" He smiled. "I guess we have more in common than you'd like to admit."

Books by Brenda Minton

Love Inspired

Trusting Him
His Little Cowgirl
A Cowboy's Heart
The Cowboy Next Door
Rekindled Hearts
Blessings of the Season
  "The Christmas Letter"
Jenna's Cowboy Hero
The Cowboy's Courtship
The Cowboy's Sweetheart
Thanksgiving Groom
The Cowboy's Family
The Cowboy's Homecoming

Christmas Gifts
  *"Her Christmas Cowboy"
*The Cowboy's Holiday
  Blessing*
The Bull Rider's Baby
The Rancher's Secret Wife
The Cowboy's Healing Ways
The Cowboy Lawman
The Boss's Bride
*The Cowboy's Christmas
  Courtship*
The Cowboy's Reunited Family
Single Dad Cowboy

*Cooper Creek

BRENDA MINTON

started creating stories to entertain herself during hour-long rides on the school bus. In high school she wrote romance novels to entertain her friends. The dream grew and so did her aspirations to become an author. She started with notebooks, handwritten manuscripts and characters who refused to go away until their stories were told. Eventually she put away the pen and paper and got down to business with the computer. The journey took a few years, with some encouragement and rejection along the way—as well as a lot of stubbornness on her part. In 2006 her dream to write for Love Inspired Books came true. Brenda lives in the rural Ozarks with her husband, three kids and an abundance of cats and dogs. She enjoys a chaotic life that she wouldn't trade for anything—except, on occasion, a beach house in Texas. You can stop by and visit at her website, www.brendaminton.net.

Single Dad Cowboy
Brenda Minton

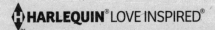

Recycling programs
for this product may
not exist in your area.

™ LOVE INSPIRED BOOKS

ISBN-13: 978-0-373-87890-1

SINGLE DAD COWBOY

www.Harlequin.com

Printed in U.S.A.

When you pass through the waters,
I will be with you; and when you pass through
the rivers, they will not sweep over you.
When you walk through the fire, you will not be burned;
the flames will not set you ablaze.
—*Isaiah* 43:2

To Hannah.

And to the readers of Cooper Creek, for the emails,
the encouragement and prayers along the way.
I hope you enjoy Dylan's story.

A big "thank you" to my editor Melissa Endlich
for her wisdom and patience.

Chapter One

The farmer stood his ground, his jeans loose, his button-down shirt frayed, with one button missing. Harmony Cross didn't back down, though. She couldn't back down. She also couldn't explain why the horse in his corral mattered so much to her. But the skinny Appaloosa, black with a smattering of white on its rump, mattered. Possibly more than anything had ever mattered in her whole life.

She needed this horse. She needed something to pour her heart into, something that would love her in return and maybe, just maybe, help her find a way back to the person she used to be.

"I don't know why you think I'm not taking care of that animal." The old farmer, with a gray grizzled beard and sunken, hazy brown eyes, scratched his chin, as if he really didn't get it. "I just rode him in the rodeo last night."

"No, you didn't," Harmony countered, nearly smiling, yet not. "I'll give you double what the animal is worth."

"I'm not selling that horse. He's a national champion."

Harmony glanced at the skin-and-bones animal. "No, he isn't. I've been driving by here for a week, and every day that horse is reaching across the fence trying to get one blade of grass. He's starving."

He pointed a finger at her that trembled. "I don't care if you are Gibson Cross's kid. You aren't going to talk to me that way, missy."

So, he knew who she was. Even though she'd tried to keep a low profile since she showed up in Dawson, Oklahoma, a week ago there would always be talk. There would always be people wanting to help. There would always be people who thought they knew where her life had gone wrong and what she needed to do to get back on track.

She'd come here looking for a place to hide, to get her life together because no one knew how much she hurt inside. The physical pain was nothing compared to the heartache of losing her best friend, the guilt that plagued her daily, and the nightmares.

At twenty-six, finding herself didn't come easy.

At twenty-six, she had a list. Not a bucket list, but a list for moving forward. First, stay clean. Second, be physically whole again. Third, find a place to be herself, without everyone trying to help. Fourth, stay clean. And fifth—somehow come to terms with the fact that Amy would never call her again.

The horse had been an impulsive thing; it didn't really fit into her plans. Each time she drove by the farm, she saw the animal. And each time her heart got a little more involved. This time she'd stopped. She looked from the horse to Mr. Tanner.

"Look, the horse is just in that corral doing nothing but grazing rocks and dirt." She softened her voice to one of sympathy. Because she did feel bad for the farmer who lived in the tiny square of a house, the front porch sagging on one end. He looked as hungry as his horse. Selling the animal to her could mean money he didn't have, maybe buying groceries he needed. So why was he being so stubborn? She wanted to ask, but knew the question would set him off again.

"I know what that horse is doing. He's waiting for my grandson to come home to work with him. I'm not selling."

"Maybe your grandson has outgrown the animal. It happens. They start looking at girls, driving cars, and horses lose their importance." It had happened to her. She tried not to let the memories slide back into her mind, memories of losing herself. Somewhere along the way, she'd lost the horse-crazy girl who loved to run barrels, build a bonfire and sing in church. The girl who knew herself.

That girl had lost herself in a life far from Dawson.

The old man, Mr. Tanner, shook his head and moisture filled the hazy brown eyes. "Get out of here."

"Mr. Tanner, I just want…"

He moved toward her, taking a quick step, grabbing her arm with a hand that shook. "Get back in that shiny car of yours and go. The horse isn't for sale."

Time for a new tactic. "Then I won't buy him. I'll take him to my place and feed him. Your grandson can come and see him if he decides he likes horses again."

Mr. Tanner brushed at his eyes and shook his head. "Terry died in Afghanistan."

Harmony closed her eyes briefly as a wave of grief slid through her heart. "I'm so sorry."

A truck pulled up the drive. A dinged and dented extended-cab truck that she didn't recognize. It rolled to a stop. The man inside sat there a minute, his hat pulled low over his eyes.

"Just what we need is a Cooper showing up and butting into my business," Mr. Tanner growled, giving her a narrow-eyed look.

"I didn't invite him," she tossed back.

Harmony turned toward the truck and the cowboy getting out. She was suddenly tired, and her body was starting to react to standing for so long. She hadn't thought this would be so difficult, buying a skin-and-bones horse. Nothing had been easy since the accident a little less than a year ago.

New Year's Eve would mark the one-year anniversary. It wasn't an anniversary she wanted to celebrate. New Year's Eve would never be a fun-filled holiday again. She would never bring in another year without thinking of that phone call, asking her best friend to pick her up because she was so drunk she couldn't drive.

"Dylan Cooper, been a mite too long since I seen you in these parts." Mr. Tanner's words shook her back to the present. She looked up as Dylan Cooper walked with a slow, easy gait in their direction.

Harmony wanted to groan but didn't. Dylan Cooper was the last person she needed to see. She'd heard he was living in Texas. Of course he would be home now. Of course he would still be the best-looking Cooper of the bunch, with his lean cowboy frame and country-boy grin. He was tanned from summer sunshine. And his dark hair curled beneath his white cowboy hat.

With a dozen kids in Angie and Tim Cooper's family, calling him the best-looking was saying something. In this new life she didn't have time for good-looking, smooth-talking men. She had two relationships she was focusing on. With herself, and with God.

"Bill." Dylan Cooper adjusted his cowboy hat and shifted to look at her. Harmony lifted her chin a notch and stared right back at him. The hazel eyes she remembered from so long ago were less teasing, less sharp. He had gone from boy to man in the years since she'd seen him last.

The teenage Dylan had been a flirt. He'd been too cute for words and he'd known it. She had steered clear. But then one year she'd taken a walk down by the creek with him. He'd kissed her, told her he didn't like spoiled little girls and then walked away, leaving her mad enough to spit.

"Harmony Cross, I didn't expect to see you here." His gaze lowered to the cane in her right hand and then eased back to her face. "How are you?"

"Good." She stopped herself from being sarcastic. She'd had a wreck that nearly killed her and did kill her best friend. She'd been in rehab. She'd overcome addiction. She was great. "How are you?"

"Been better." He shifted back to Bill Tanner. "You doing all right, Bill?"

"Been better." Bill smiled just a little as he repeated Dylan's words, but Harmony saw the moisture in his eyes.

"I just came to pay my respects. I'm real sorry, Bill. If there's anything you and Doris need, you let me know."

"I appreciate that, Dylan. We're making it, though."

"What's Miss Cross doing here?" Dylan didn't look at her. He adjusted his white cowboy hat and kept his gaze fixed on Mr. Tanner.

"She's trying to buy Terry's horse." Mr. Tanner sighed and shook his head. "All of this fuss over a horse."

"Mr. Tanner, at least let me buy you some hay." Harmony made the quick offer, thinking now would be the time to escape.

"Why are you keeping that horse, Bill?" Dylan's tone was easy, friendly. Harmony shot him a look, doubting he was really on her side in this matter. More likely he was on the horse's side.

Mr. Tanner looked away from them, back to the horse in the corral. The animal, as if he knew they were discussing his future, moved to the fence to watch. It was mid-September and a breeze blew, feathering the horse's dark tail in the light wind. For a minute the animal was almost pretty.

"I keep thinking he'll come home." Mr. Tanner finally answered, the words hollow and sad.

Dylan's hand rested on the farmer's shoulder. "Terry wouldn't want his horse kept that way."

"I know."

Harmony waited, holding her breath while Bill Tanner looked from her to the horse. Her gaze strayed to Dylan Cooper and he smiled. The lingering sadness in his eyes took her by surprise.

But she was more surprised when she noticed the door of his truck opening. As Dylan talked to Bill Tanner, two children escaped from his truck. A little girl, maybe preschool age, barefoot and wearing shorts and a tank top. And a boy, just a toddler. Both had blond hair. The boy's hair was buzzed short. The girl's hair was in raggedy braids with wisps of hair coming loose. The two held hands as they sneaked across the yard.

If Dylan had known Harmony Cross would be at the Tanners', he would have ignored the voice in his head telling him to stop and pay his respects to Bill and Doris Tanner over the loss of the grandson they'd raised. Harmony Cross, with her dark blue eyes and curly blond hair framing her pretty face, was the last thing he needed in his life right now. He barely had time for himself these days, let alone thoughts that took him down back roads of the past.

What he needed had everything to do with the two kids in his truck.

As Harmony stood there, leaning heavily on a cane, waiting for Bill Tanner to come to his senses, Dylan gave her a long look. He remembered the last time he'd seen her. She'd been pretty full of herself back then. That girl seemed to be long gone. She'd been through a lot recently.

Hadn't they all?

He guessed back in the day they'd all thought they'd live charmed lives free from trouble.

At least his personal drama hadn't made the national news. Just the Dawson gossip channels. He guessed that might be nearly as bad. He'd been home a few weeks, and everywhere he went people asked questions. Or mentioned a sweet girl that he should meet. Because marriage would solve his problems?

Harmony was no longer watching him. Her gaze had shot past him and he saw a flicker of a smile turn her lips. She bit down on her bottom lip and her gaze flicked back to him like she hadn't seen a thing. And that made him mighty curious. He turned just as Cash and Callie hurried across the yard toward a kitten that had crawled out from under the house.

The door of the house banged shut just as Callie pounced on the kitten that fortunately had the good sense to run back under the porch. Doris Tanner walked onto the porch, a thin woman in dark blue housedress. He remembered when she used to bake the best pies in the state. She shook her head as she walked down the steps, holding the rail for support.

Dylan shot her a smile as he hurried and scooped the adventurers up, one under each arm. He'd gotten pretty good at keeping them corralled. Sometimes he forgot that they were escape artists. Doris smiled his way and stepped next to her husband.

Dylan settled a kid on each hip and thought about making his own escape. But he didn't want to leave Doris refereeing the two people that looked like they might butt heads any moment.

"Why all of this fuss over a skinny old horse?" Doris reached for Bill's arm. "The horse needs to go, Billy. We can't keep him in that corral forever."

"Terry said to keep his horse. His last words to me were telling me I shouldn't sell his horse while he was gone. I talked to him the day before…" Bill looked at the horse, shaking his head. Dylan wondered if anyone else felt the pain in the air, thick, heavy, weighing down on this family and this farm.

They still had a few days until autumn's official start, but the air was a little cooler today and the breeze came from the north. There was still green grass and leaves on the trees, thanks to some good rain. At the Tanner farm, everything seemed gray. Dylan guessed he recognized it because he'd been feeling the same way for the past few months, since Katrina passed away. The two of them hadn't ever been more than friends, but she'd needed someone at her side during the last year. Her last year. And she'd been only twenty-six.

"Mr. Tanner, I'm so sorry." Harmony spoke and Dylan drifted back to the present. Harmony's hand rested on Bill's arm and her gaze connected with Doris's. The two women smiled at each other.

"Take the horse." Mr. Tanner turned and walked away.

"I don't think…" Harmony turned to look at Dylan. He shrugged. She was on her own. Cash and Callie were struggling to get down and he knew they wanted that kitten.

He was settling them back on the ground when the kitten came out from under the porch again and headed across the yard. Harmony leaned down and picked it up. She gave the flea-bitten tabby a sad look and handed it to Callie.

"Take the horse, honey." Doris Tanner patted Harmony's arm. "He's just a reminder. I want him gone. I want the corral gone. And Dylan, let those kids have that kitten."

Harmony nodded and then flicked at tears streaming down her cheeks. "I'll write you a check."

Dylan watched as Harmony made painful steps back to her car. She sat in the driver's seat and more tears trickled down her cheeks. Was it was from physical pain or from sharing heartache with the Tanners? He guessed when she showed up today, she expected to find a relieved farmer ready to take a check for a skinny horse, and never would have guessed at the pain she'd find.

She pushed herself out of the car and walked back to Doris Tanner. Bill had gone back in the house. Harmony handed over the check and Doris looked at it and shook her head.

"That old horse isn't worth that much money." Doris tried to hand the check back.

"He's a national champion." Harmony smiled. They all knew it wasn't the truth. Bill had been doing his best to run her off.

"He's one step away from glue." Doris shook her head and looked at the check again.

Harmony hugged the older woman. "He's a champion to me."

For whatever reason, the rangy Appaloosa meant something to Harmony Cross, and Dylan didn't want to know why. He sure didn't want to see her as someone who cared about other people. That made her too big a complication. And with Callie and Cash heading for the truck with a kitten, he was pretty sure he had all the complications he could handle. What he needed was space to breathe, to figure out how to be a single dad.

"Do you have someone who can haul him for you?" Doris asked, and for whatever reason she glanced his way.

Harmony ignored him. "I'll find someone."

"I need to hit the road. Doris, if you all need anything, you give me a call."

"Thank you, Dylan. But I think you've probably got your hands full as it is. Bill and I are making it through this. We've made it through plenty in our lives."

"I'm just down the road." Dylan glanced over his

shoulder to make sure the kids were back in the truck. "And thanks for the kitten."

At that, Doris smiled. "Oh, Dylan, kids need animals. It keeps them smiling, and don't we all need to smile?"

"Yeah, I guess we do." He really didn't like cats. But it was pointless to mention that.

Doris touched his arm. "I'm going on in to see about Bill. Will you help her find someone to haul that horse out of here? And if you want that round pen, take it."

"Sure thing, Doris."

Harmony stood at the corral trying to coax that skinny horse to her with a few blades of grass she'd plucked from the yard. The horse trotted to the far side of the round pen, wanting nothing to do with her or that fistful of grass. He waited until Doris entered the house, then he walked up to the round pen. It didn't make sense to have the horse in that pen. Bill had land. He had cattle. The whole situation smelled of grief and pain.

"I'll haul him over to your place." The offer slipped out, because it was the right thing to do. Harmony turned, smiling as she brushed hair back from her face.

"I can find someone."

Argumentative females. He sighed. "Harmony, I'll haul the horse."

Harmony held her hand out and the horse brushed against her palm and then backed away. He didn't think the animal had been worked since Terry left for the military a couple of years ago.

"He's a lot of horse," he cautioned. "He isn't even halter-broke."

"I'm not worried about it."

"I'd hate to see you mess around and get hurt."

She shot him a look, and he realized she was holding on to the fence, holding herself up. Stubborn female. He didn't have time for stubborn.

"Why don't you get in your car and head back to your place? I'll get a trailer and bring him over to you this afternoon. You'll have to pen him up for a few days because in this condition he's likely to founder if he gets too much green grass."

"I'll put him in the small corral by the barn. It has plenty of grass for now." She smiled at him. Man, that smile, it was something else. It could knock a guy to his knees. "And I'll take that offer to haul him for me. If it isn't too much trouble. The kids—"

He cut her off. "How much did you pay for him?"

"That's a business deal, Mr. Cooper. I don't sign checks and tell." She turned away from the horse and made slow, painful steps back to her car.

He opened the car door for her. "That was real nice of you."

She slid into the seat and looked up at him. "Why not do something for someone if you have the chance? That's what you've been doing, isn't it?"

He rested his arm on the top of her Audi and looked in at her. He knew she was referring to Cash and Callie, Katrina's kids. "Yeah, I guess we're all grown-up now."

"Right, of course we are." She started her car and reached for the door, forcing him to back up. "I'll see you this afternoon."

He watched as she closed the door, and took off down the drive. Bill Tanner was standing on his front porch. The old guy walked down the steps, a little bow-legged from years in the saddle. He'd been a saddle bronc rider back in the day, one of the best.

He'd taught Dylan a thing or two about the sport. Dylan and Terry had both ridden saddle bronc, before Terry had signed up for the army. Dylan glanced at the rangy horse and smiled, because Terry had bought the animal from a stock provider who had intended to use him in rodeos and then decided the horse didn't have enough buck.

But he still had plenty of buck, and if Harmony Cross gentled the animal down, she deserved a medal.

"Well, I guess Terry's horse is going to have a good home." Bill walked up to the round pen. "I should have sold him a long time ago. I'm just a stubborn old man who doesn't like to deal with reality."

"It isn't easy, this reality stuff," Dylan admitted.

"Take the girl her check back." Bill held out the check with the flowery signature and four digits.

"Nah, Bill, I think she'd be real upset if you sent that back. Keep it and take Doris to the beach."

Bill grinned. Probably one of his first real smiles in a long time. "It don't seem right, to have this much money in my hand. But the beach would sure be nice."

"Go. Have a good time." Dylan adjusted his hat to block the sun. "She ain't gonna miss the money, Bill."

"No, I reckon she won't. She was sure determined to get that animal. I guess she'll be good to him. I just didn't want to sell him and have someone put him back in the arena. Terry thought there was more to the horse than that. Something about his eyes."

"Maybe she sees it, too."

"Maybe." Bill wore a baseball cap with a big fish emblem on the front. "Guess I'll go fishing."

"Don't forget to do something with Doris."

"She won't let me forget." Bill started to go back inside but stopped, and looked from the truck to Dylan. "You'll get through this, Dylan."

"Yeah, I guess I will."

When he got in his truck, he looked at the two kids in the backseat. Cash was in his car seat. Callie was sitting in her big-kid booster seat. She reminded him often that she was four and Cash was just a baby.

She was holding tight to her kitten and the thing looked like it might be about ready to let loose with its claws.

"That kitten isn't happy, Callie." He grabbed a jacket and handed it back to her. "Wrap him up before you get scratched."

"He's happy," she insisted as she wrapped the jacket around the hissing feline.

"Of course she is. You know I don't like cats, right?" He glanced in the rearview mirror as he pulled onto the road. And he also didn't like getting involved in Harmony Cross's life. He had enough on his plate.

"You'll like this one, Dylan," Callie informed him with a big smile.

"What do you think, Cash? I need a guy on my side."

Cash, not quite two, responded with one of his drooling, toothy grins and said, "Cat."

"Yeah, cat." Dylan shook his head and headed for town. One of these days he'd have to figure out how his ability to say *no* had gotten broken to the point of no repair.

If he'd figured it out sooner, he might not have offered to haul that horse for Harmony Cross.

The one thing, actually two, that he didn't regret were sitting in the backseat of his truck. Cash and Callie, the children of his late friend. She'd lost a battle with cancer, and he'd done the only thing he had known he could do for her. He'd agreed to raise her kids because there hadn't been anyone else.

One year ago he'd decided to help out a friend. Now he was a single dad.

Chapter Two

Harmony stood in the old barn that had been a part of the Cross Ranch for as long as she could remember. Her parents had bought the place twenty years ago, when her dad had first made a name for himself in Nashville. They'd wanted a place to go where life was still normal. Where the Cross kids could be kids and the family could do what other families did. Attending church on Sunday, rodeos and the local diner.

And because Harmony needed to find that part of herself that still believed in something, in who she was, or wanted to be, she had returned to Dawson and to the old farmhouse with all of its good memories.

She loved this place because it hadn't changed. No matter what else happened in life, this house remained the same. Her parents had updated it, but they'd kept it as original as possible. The barn was solid with red-painted wood siding, a hayloft, a few stalls and a chicken pen off the back. The chicken pen was empty, and there hadn't been animals in the barn for years. There were cows in the field only because the Coopers leased the land.

Even though the barn had stood empty, it still smelled

of cedar, straw and farm animals. Today there would be a horse. She smiled as she opened one of the few stalls. It had a door that led to the corral and it was roomy.

She'd found one bale of straw, probably left over from the fall decorating her mother had done the previous year. She broke up the bale and scattered a few flakes in the stall for bedding.

After she'd left the Tanner's she'd stopped at the feed store in Dawson and ordered some grain and hay to be delivered. It was already stacked in the feed room. She was all set. But her heart was a little jittery as she thought about what she was taking on and why. She knew the dangers of getting involved with Dylan Cooper. Her heart couldn't handle his charm, and she knew he was best left alone. Her dad used to say the same thing about poisonous plants and poisonous snakes. *Leave well enough alone and you won't get hurt,* he'd warn.

In the peaceful country stillness she heard a trailer rattling up the driveway. She stepped out of the stall, closing the door behind her. When she walked out of the barn, Dylan nodded a greeting as he pulled past her.

He backed the trailer up to the gate of the corral. The horse stomped and whinnied his displeasure at being moved. Harmony stepped a little closer as the truck stopped moving. The horse pushed his nose out of an opening of the trailer and whinnied again.

"It's okay, boy, we'll get you fattened up and you'll be happy to be here." She reached to pet his nose and he pulled back. She got it; look but don't touch.

"You think he's going to be all happy that you rescued him?" Dylan walked around the trailer and opened the gate. "Because all men fall at your feet, Harmony Cross?"

"Maybe I was wrong, maybe you haven't changed."

He smiled a little and she saw the lurking sadness again.

"Oh, I think we've both changed." He swung the back of the trailer open. "And I'm sorry for baiting you that way. Old habits and all."

"You're right. Maybe we should call a truce?"

A truce? They'd had an adversarial relationship for years. He'd once loosened the cinch on her saddle just to watch it slide as she tried to get on her horse. She'd put mud in his boots. All in good fun. But it had gone a long way in cementing their relationship.

A truce would mean, what? Being friends? The idea felt a little bit dangerous.

The horse wasn't coming out of the trailer. Dylan backed up and whistled. The poor animal stood his ground, trembling. Harmony stepped a little closer and spoke softly. The horse listened, his ears twitching and his head moving just the slightest bit to look at her.

"I'm not sure exactly why we need a truce," Dylan said as he stepped up into the trailer and reached for the gelding's tail. "Come on, Beau, head on out of there."

"His name is Beau?"

Dylan nodded, stepping back and pulling a little on the scraggly black tail. The gelding backed out of the trailer, his hooves clanking on the floor. When he hit firm ground he turned and trotted across the corral. He might have kept going but he noticed the green grass and immediately lowered his head and started to graze. He would pull at a mouthful of grass, and then look around at his new surroundings, ears twitching.

"He'll settle in." Dylan closed the back of the trailer and then the gate. "You understand you can't ride him."

"You understand that I'm very aware of what I can and can't do."

"Is that your idea of a truce?" He shook his head and exhaled loudly with obvious impatience. "I don't mean to tell you what you physically can and can't do. I'm telling you, that horse can't be ridden."

"Why?"

"Why are you so defensive?" he countered.

She watched the horse for a minute. From inside the truck she heard the lilting voice of the little girl, her Texas accent a welcome distraction.

"Well?" He pushed for an answer.

"Because I'm here to get away from people who feel I need to be told at every turn what I can and can't do. Since I got home from the Tanners', I've had three phone calls. One from your mother, one from my mother and one from my older brother. I've been warned three times that I have to be careful with the horse."

"So what you're saying is, you've had all of the advice you can handle for a lifetime?" He smiled. "I guess we have more in common than you'd like to admit."

She didn't want common ground. "So, about this horse…"

"He was a saddle bronc horse that Terry bought from a stock contractor. Terry had ideas that this horse was special."

They both looked at the dark horse with the white splotch on his rump and little to recommend him other than a pretty-shaped head and nice eyes, even if they were a little wild at the moment.

"Well, whatever the reason he bought Beau, I'm glad

he did. Beau might not be all that special, but I think we need each other."

"It happens that way sometimes." He glanced at his watch and then there was a cry from his truck. "I have to go."

"What are their names?" She should have let him leave but she followed him to the truck. There was something about his situation that gave them a bond.

"Callie, she's four. Cash is almost two." He looked in the window at the two kids in the backseat.

Harmony stepped close to his side to get a better view. Cash smiled past the thumb in his mouth. Callie gave her a seriously angry look. The little girl still held that kitten from Bill and Doris Tanner's. Both kids watched them with big blue eyes. They were sweet, perfectly sweet.

And he was raising them. Alone.

"I'm sure your family is a lot of help." She meant it as a good thing. He gave her a serious look.

"I don't know, do you consider your family trying to help a good thing?"

She shrugged and her attention refocused on the two kids in the back of his truck. "It can be. And sometimes it's overwhelming."

"Yeah, exactly. I know they mean well, but sometimes a person needs to be able to breathe and think about their next step."

Maybe they had more in common than she'd realized. "That's why I came to Dawson," she admitted, "but it seems I can't escape, because even here there's a steady stream of people knocking on my door."

Not that she didn't appreciate the offers. She really did.

Dylan reached for the door of his truck but paused,

his hand dropping to his side. He smiled and she didn't know what to think. His smile worried her. And it shifted her off balance. All at the same time.

She needed all the balance she could get these days.

"We could throw them off our scent, you know."

"What does that mean?" She really shouldn't have asked. She knew Dylan. As a kid she'd gotten in trouble more than once because she'd gone along with his crazy schemes.

"We could team up. If they think we're in each other's lives, helping each other out, they might back off."

It took her a minute to really get the meaning of his plan, then she shook her head. "You must really think I'm desperate if you think I'm going to pretend we're in a relationship."

"I don't think you're desperate, Princess." He used the old nickname and winked. "I just think that you'd like a little peace and quiet to get your life together. Like me. I've been taking care of Cash and Callie by myself for a year, but now that I'm back in town, people think I don't know one end of a diaper from the other."

"I have to admit I wouldn't think you knew that."

He laughed easily, something that she envied. "I'm a Cooper, Harmony. I have eleven siblings. Our home has been the stopping point for more foster children than I can count and I have tons of nieces and nephews. Of course I can change a diaper. My mom never believed in separate duties for the males and females in our family. She's an equal-opportunity chore giver."

There was a lot to admire about Angie Cooper, a lady who could command a family as large as hers with love and grace. Harmony's own mother was just as loving, but a family of three children had seemed tiny compared to the Coopers.

"So?" Dylan nudged her arm.

"No. There is no way I'm going to 'team up' with you." There was no way she could handle Dylan in her life. Her heart couldn't handle it if she let him down. Or those two children. She'd hurt too many people already. The other reason would make more sense to him. "Dylan, I'm working hard to be a recovering addict. And one of the goals for myself is no lying."

"I'm not asking you to lie. I'm offering an exchange of services. I'll be here to help you out when you need me. And you help me out from time to time. Everyone is satisfied. And I'll no longer be pegged as the bachelor in town most in need of a wife."

"I think the answer is still no."

He sniffed his shirt. "But why? I don't smell bad."

"You're nothing but trouble, Dylan Cooper."

"I promise, no one is going to ground us." He reached for the truck door again. "Think about it. We don't have to lie. We just have to team up. We've already called a truce, right? So if we help each other out, that's a handy excuse when someone calls to check on us. You can say Dylan has it covered. I can say you're helping with the kids."

"And I'm still saying no. I'm here if you need me, but needing space is about needing space."

He climbed up inside the beat-up old truck cab and started the engine. "I'll see you around then, Princess."

She stepped back and watched him drive off. No, she wouldn't see him around. She was going to hibernate here on the ranch and give herself time to find her life again. She wasn't in Dawson to get involved in the lives of the people she'd once known. The last thing she needed in her current condition was a distraction.

Dylan Cooper, with his hazel eyes and bad-boy smile was just that, a distraction. His dark, curly hair was a distraction. His swagger, all cowboy with faded jeans, also a distraction.

She walked back to the corral, proud of the way she'd made it through the day. Each day got easier. She used the cane less. She cried less. More and more she believed she might survive. Today she'd managed to smile more. She'd even laughed.

Because of Dylan and those two children. She could admit he'd brought a lightness she hadn't felt in a long time. Because Dylan didn't allow her to be a victim.

In the first few months after the accident, she'd wanted to die. She'd wanted to give up. She'd found ways to numb herself to the physical pain, and to the emotional pain that often hurt worse.

Her best friend had been driving the night of the car accident because Harmony hadn't been sober enough to get behind the wheel. She stood at the corral watching the horse graze on what grass there was in the small enclosure. It wasn't enough to hurt him. She'd have the vet come out tomorrow to check him and make sure he didn't need more than grass and grain.

Beau turned to look at her, his ears twitching as he sniffed the air. She whistled softly and he took a few steps in her direction but the grass distracted him again.

It didn't take long for her back and legs to give out. Harmony limped back into the barn and sat down on an upturned bucket. She leaned her head against the wall and waited for the pain to subside, at least enough to make it to the house. Her mind filled with thoughts of Amy. She kept her eyes open, because if she closed them she would see the flash of lights as a truck ran a stop sign. She would hear the crash of metal and see her friend, lifeless in the driver's seat.

In the silence her heart moved toward God, praying for peace and strength to get through.

When she finally walked out of the barn, the sun was a hazy fixture hanging in the western sky. As she crossed the lawn toward the house, she heard a child laughing and realized it came from the little house just across the field from her place. The house sat on Cooper land. And even from a distance she could see Dylan Cooper in the front yard.

She watched them, smiling when Dylan lifted Callie to his shoulders. She could hear the faint laughter, carried on the breeze. A truck pulled up her drive and stopped. She smiled at Wyatt Johnson, pastor of Dawson Community Church, and his wife, Rachel. It was their second visit this week. She knew she had her dad to thank for that. Since getting to town she'd also had visits from various members of the Cooper family.

"Hi, Wyatt, Rachel," she greeted them as they got out of their truck.

"We were on our way home from town and thought we'd stop by and see if you need anything." Wyatt's gaze fixed on the corral and his eyes narrowed. "Is that the horse from over at Bill Tanner's? Terry's horse?"

"It is." She looked back at the horse that hadn't stopped grazing since they unloaded him.

"How did you manage that?"

She shrugged, telling him the short version of the story. The version that didn't include Dylan. "I think Bill realized it was time to let the horse go."

Rachel moved next to her husband. "And the memories."

"Yes, the memories." Harmony smiled.

"We wanted to check on you and make sure everything is okay out here. If you need anything at all, let us know." Wyatt made the same offer he'd made days ago when she first arrived in Dawson.

"I know where to find you," Harmony repeated her line from that conversation. "And church starts at eleven."

Rachel smiled at that. "I think she's got it, Wyatt."

"I know she does." Wyatt shrugged and looked a little sheepish. "But you're here alone and your dad…"

A guilty flush tinted his cheeks.

"My dad wants to make sure I'm okay. I know."

Wyatt didn't smile this time. "We're all family here, Harmony. I think we all want to know that you're okay."

"I appreciate that, Wyatt, I really do. And I promise I'll call if I need anything."

He slipped an arm around his wife. Harmony felt the tiniest twinge of envy at the easy gesture. She wondered how it would feel to be part of a couple, part of a team. But she wouldn't know because she wouldn't allow herself a relationship, not a real one, not for a very long time. Not until she was positive she could do this life thing without letting anyone else down.

Rachel stepped away from Wyatt and gave her a quick hug. "I'm just about a mile down the road if you ever want coffee."

"That's an invitation I won't turn down. Thank you." She heard the quick laughter from across the field, Dylan and the children again. She pretended not to notice and smiled at the couple standing in front of her.

"And Dylan came by earlier. He offered to help out if I need anything. It just made sense, because we live so close."

Wyatt gave her a steady, questioning look and she wanted to look away. Of course Wyatt, long a resident of Dawson, remembered her adversarial relationship with Dylan Cooper. She smiled and hoped he wouldn't ask questions.

"That's good of Dylan. He's had a lot on his shoulders and I'm sure he could use the help, too."

"He seems to be handling parenthood." The easy words slipped out, because it was the truth. "But I'm here if he needs anything."

Wyatt's face wavered between curious and concerned, but he shrugged and then offered an easy smile. "There's another reason I stopped by today."

"Okay."

"I want to start a recovery program."

Harmony bit down on her lip and nodded, unsure what to say. She was involved in a program that offered anonymity. She craved it because for a long time it seemed as if everyone knew that Harmony Cross was addicted to prescription drugs. Did they know how easy it was to get those drugs? A toothache, headache, stomach pain, the list was endless. No one really asked questions. No one delved deeper. And when the prescriptions ran out, an addict knew how to find the person with pills to sell.

"Harmony, I know this is tough." Wyatt had shifted his arm from his wife's waist and now held her hand but his direct gaze focused on Harmony's face. "I know that you came here to shed the focus people were putting on your life, the attention and probably some suffocation by people who mean well."

She smiled at that. "You *have* talked to my parents."

"I understand how much you want to hide and how much you want people to stop asking if they can help or if you're okay."

"Bingo." She hoped that didn't sound too harsh. She knew Wyatt's first wife had committed suicide, leaving him to raise two little girls alone and deal with the loss of a woman he loved.

"It isn't easy to get back to life." Wyatt looked down at Rachel. "Sometimes we need a person who leads us back into the light."

"I'm not looking for a person." The answer came easily. "I'm not ready for relationships. I'm not ready to step in front of a group of well-meaning church people and tell them I'm an addict."

"I think you'll find this group of people pretty supportive and ready to help each other through some tough times."

"I know," she said. "But I need time. I've had all of the sermons thrown at me. God allowed this to happen to get me back in church. Or if I hadn't walked away from God, this wouldn't have happened." The one that hurt the most was that God had a reason for taking her best friend. Not her. "I believe, Wyatt, I've just had a pretty big crisis in faith. I was hoping if I came back here…"

Wyatt filled in the rest. "That God would be waiting?"

"Something like that. I thought I'd find the old Harmony, the person I used to be."

"I think you will. I remember her as a girl who never backed down."

She hoped she'd be that person again. "The one question I really need answered is, why Amy? Why not me?"

She hadn't planned to say the words out loud. She shook her head, blinking away the quick sting of tears. Wyatt started toward her but she backed away because one touch and she'd lose it, the way she'd been close to losing it for days. Amy, her best friend, had been one of the kindest, most decent people Harmony had known.

"No one on this earth has that answer, Harmony, and I'm not going to try to guess the reason. But I do know that God has a plan for your life, and that plan isn't for you to give up."

"Thank you." She wiped at her eyes and managed a weak smile. "I'm not sure if I can say I'm glad you stopped by."

"I don't blame you. And I'll let you know when we start this group. In case you change your mind."

And then they left, waving goodbye as they climbed in the truck.

She waved back and headed for the house. She made it to the front porch and sat down on one of the old rocking chairs that had been recently painted a pretty poppy color. Her mother loved bright colors.

The chairs matched the brightly colored geraniums and gerbera daisies blooming in the flower beds. Everything looked cheerful. It looked the way it had years ago when she'd spent happy summers here.

She rocked, enjoying the soft, late summer breeze that blew across the porch, cooling the air. There were no more sounds of laughter from across the field.

Only silence.

For a moment it felt like peace. And in the midst of that peace she remembered that she had just aligned herself with Dylan Cooper. She guessed eventually she'd have to tell him that she was accepting his offer.

Dylan pulled in to the parking lot of the Mad Cow Café and immediately spotted the Audi driven by Harmony Cross. The only empty space was next to the silver car. He groaned to himself, because if he groaned out loud, he'd have to explain why to Callie. These days she asked a lot of questions. Her favorite words were *why* and *what* and *how.*

When he'd left Harmony an hour earlier, he hadn't expected to see her back in town so soon.

"Dylan, why are you frowning?"

He glanced in the rearview mirror and smiled at the little girl that he'd known since she was a baby. She smiled back. He couldn't hide anything from her. She was always watching and saw a lot more than most kids.

"No reason. Just wondering what I'm going to have for supper. What do you want?"

"Chicken strips. And Cash wants tater tots and green beans."

"Green beans?" He laughed. "Why do you get chicken strips and he has to eat the green beans?"

"Because he's little." She said it with the appropriate roll of her eyes that basically told him even a moron would know that a little kid needed green beans.

"I think you should both eat green beans." He climbed out of the truck and pushed the seat forward to reach in the back. He really needed to get a car or a new truck, one with an extended cab and four doors. The two doors had been fine when it had been just him and a dog traveling around the country.

Car seats and kids changed everything.

He unbuckled Cash from his seat and Callie unbuckled herself. She came in real handy, that kid did. She was his little helper. He hiked Cash onto his hip and reached to help Callie down from the truck. Together the three of them headed toward the diner. And then he heard the door of the Audi open. He hadn't realized she'd still been sitting in that car.

He watched her climb out of that car like it took every last ounce of strength she had to move. A wounded Harmony Cross was the last thing he needed right now. He'd been at Katrina's side for the past year, and everything inside him was pretty much wrung out like an old kitchen rag. He had enough energy for himself and the two kids she'd left him to raise. Her kids, not his. But they were his now and he wouldn't let them down.

Katrina's husband had died in a truck accident coming home from a long haul to California. He'd been heading to Katrina's side as she'd gone into labor with Cash.

As much as he wanted to ignore Harmony and walk into the Mad Cow, he waited, watching Harmony's painful steps across the parking lot. Her long, curling blond hair was pulled back in a ponytail and she had changed from jeans and a T-shirt to a sundress. The stubborn female had left her cane in the car. He saw the grimace of pain around her mouth. He saw the flinch with each step.

"Are you trying to get your picture put in the dictionary next to stubborn?" he asked as he waited.

She looked up as if she hadn't noticed them there. Her gaze landed on Callie, not him, and she smiled. Man, she was thin. He hadn't noticed earlier. He'd had more on his mind than Harmony and her too-skinny horse. He guessed they both needed fattening up. But saying that would definitely break the truce between them.

"I'm not stubborn." She shifted her eyes from Callie to him. She was still pretty. Tired-looking, but pretty. It had been a long time since he'd paid attention to a woman, but he was positive those weren't the words she wanted to hear.

"So what are you if you're not stubborn?"

"Strong." She lifted her chin as she said it, the glint in her smoky-blue eyes unmistakable.

"Right." He stuck his right elbow out for her to take hold of. "Allow me, miss."

"How very, um, chivalrous of you, Mr. Cooper." But she took his elbow, her hand holding tight. With her other hand she reached for Callie.

He guessed that's how you made a truce.

It was also how rumors got started, he realized as they walked through the front doors of the Mad Cow, the cowbell over the door clanging loud to announce their arrival. There were about a dozen customers and they all turned to watch Dylan, the kids and Harmony Cross.

Harmony dropped his arm and moved away from him. "Thanks for the lift, neighbor."

"Anytime." He watched as she retreated taking a seat in a booth. He guessed she wanted to avoid rumors, too.

He sat at a table with Callie and Cash. But his eyes

kept straying to Harmony sitting alone. She probably needed a friend. He looked at the two dirty faces sitting across from him. He had plenty of friends. And family. Cash reached for the sugar and Dylan moved it out of his way. Callie tried to slap the little guy's hand.

"Hey, Cal, let's not do that, kiddo." He smiled at her, and she wrinkled her little nose and gave him a big-eyed innocent look that said he didn't know what he was doing.

He was tired.

Cash reached for the napkins. He moved those out of the toddler's reach, too. The waitress, Breezy, headed their way with menus and the coffeepot. She smiled and easily moved everything within reach to another table. She put crayons and a coloring placemat in front of the kids and filled his cup.

"You look worn-out, Dylan."

He smiled up at her. Pretty as she was, he felt nothing but sisterly affection. After all, she was his adopted sister Mia's biological sister. And didn't that make her family?

"I'm feeling about fifty years older than I am," he admitted.

She smoothed a hand over Cash's buzzed blond hair and grinned. "Good thing you're still cute. Maybe you can find a wife to help you out with these two."

"I think I'll pass for now."

"Oh, I wasn't proposing." Breezy winked as she said that. "But I could help you find someone."

Even Breezy was in on it now. This was exactly why he'd made that proposition to Harmony.

Vera, owner of the Mad Cow Café, walked out of the

kitchen. She spotted him and headed his way. "Dylan, those are two cute babies you've got there."

"I'm *not* a baby," Callie informed Vera, her little mouth turning in a serious frown. "I'm four."

Vera took the seat next to Callie. "Well, that makes you almost grown, doesn't it? And what are you going to eat today, Sugar Plum?"

"I'm having chicken strips and fries. Cash needs green beans."

Dylan pulled off his hat and swiped a hand through hair that needed to be cut. His gaze shifted from the little girl sitting across from him to the woman on the other side of the restaurant.

He should invite her to sit with them. Even if she didn't want to take him up on his offer.

"What are you looking at, Dylan Cooper?" Vera leaned in a little. Nothing got past Vera.

"I was thinking I should invite Harmony Cross to sit with us. We have an extra chair—" the one Vera was occupying "—and she looks pretty lonely."

Vera glanced back at Harmony, then shot him a knowing look. "Is that the way the wind is blowing?"

"There ain't no wind in Oklahoma that strong, Vera. I'm just being neighborly. Could you watch these two for a minute?"

Vera laughed but nodded her agreement, and Dylan scooted his chair back and headed Harmony's direction. She looked up from the menu and glared at him as he sat down across from her.

"Eating alone isn't good for a person's digestion," he said, using an old line that had gotten him more than one date over the years. Harmony Cross just laughed.

"It's a truce, Dylan, not a courtship."

"I know that, I was just being…"

"Charming?"

For the first time in a long while, the smile on his face came easily. "Yeah, that's me, Mr. Charming."

"I don't remember that being your nickname."

"No, probably not. But you might as well join me and the kids for supper."

"Because you think you're full of good ideas. Like I didn't hear that waitress tell you she'd help you find a wife."

"Keep your voice down," he whispered. "And it is a good idea."

"It might be."

He stood up, offering her his hand and she took it. Her hand was small and soft in his. He hadn't expected to really feel anything. He definitely hadn't expected the strange surge of protectiveness or the odd urge to hold her close.

He guessed if she knew what he was thinking, she would have sat back down and refused to ever speak to him again. Instead he worked on remaining charming and nothing more. He didn't need attachments and he guessed she didn't, either.

But taking her to his table would give everyone in town the notion that he and Harmony Cross were becoming attached.

Attached.

He could tell them all, if they asked, why a man would be attached to Harmony. Or want to be attached. It would have to do with the soft hand in his, the warmth of her smile and the sweet, floral scent that wrapped him up and drew him even closer.

A green bean smacked him in the face, and that dose

of reality helped him get back to the man he knew he was. He pulled out a chair for Harmony and removed himself enough to take a deep breath.

Chapter Three

After a meal spent sitting next to Dylan as he cajoled the two children into eating vegetables, and even forced her to finish her fries, Harmony walked out the door of the Mad Cow. She knew that their departure would set off a firestorm of talk. She convinced herself she didn't care. It had been a good hour of being entertained and not thinking. It was exactly what she'd needed, in ways Dylan Cooper wouldn't have known.

The sun had set and the evening air was cooler with a breeze kicking up from the north. It didn't matter what people were saying. For tonight, Harmony had enjoyed herself.

Dylan held on to the two children, Callie and Cash. She watched him wrangle them, holding their hands and keeping calm as he led them across the parking lot.

"That wasn't so bad, was it?" he asked as he opened the truck door and hefted Cash with one arm.

"Compared to what, a tetanus shot?" she teased.

She unlocked her door and waited as he put the children in their car seats. As much as she wanted to sit down, she didn't. Instead she backed against her car and watched him lean inside the truck. His husky voice carried as he talked to the kids about bedtime and baths. He sounded for all the world like a man who had been a dad for a long time. As much as he smiled and joked, though, she'd noticed the weariness evident in his face, in eyes that looked as if they'd seen too much of life.

He finished with the kids, then mirrored her, backing against his truck as if they had all night.

He pushed his hat back and she could see his too-handsome face. Traitorous memories returned, of the one kiss they'd shared. Even though it had ended with him teasing her, it had still been a kiss a girl couldn't forget.

"So, what do you think?"

She opened her car door and sat down. If he was going to take forever, she needed a seat. "About?"

Of course she knew he meant his idea. And she had yet to tell him she'd already put his plan into action, letting Wyatt and Rachel Johnson think that Dylan's help was the only help she'd need.

He moved away from the truck and squatted next to her as she sat in her car, hitching up his jeans as he bent long legs. "Tonight worked out well. You didn't have to eat alone, dodging people asking how you're doing. I escaped more discussions on prospective wives. I saw Wyatt and Rachel Johnson's truck heading up to your place a while ago. I guess that isn't their first visit?"

"No, it isn't."

"I heard my mom say she's coming by tomorrow to check on you."

"I love your mom."

"But you don't need a daily check-in."

She smiled at that. "No, I don't."

He stood and leaned on the side of her car, bending down to look in at her. The distraction of his Old West looks, mountain-man cologne and cinnamon gum kept her from hearing what he said. She had to focus.

"You did agree to sit with me tonight."

She smiled up at him. "I might have already told Wyatt Johnson that we're helping each other out."

"Perfect. So that's it, we're an item now."

His easy statement shocked her.

"No!" The word rushed out. "I'm not interested in being half of a couple."

"Don't worry, I'm not going to buy you a ring. But I will be here if you need me. I'll help you out with that horse. I'll mow your lawn. Whatever it is people are lining up to do for you, I'm your huckleberry. And if you want to fix me a roast for dinner, that's even better."

"You think I cook now?"

"Probably not."

That hurt. "Well, I do."

He winked. "Don't get all upset, Princess, I'm teasing. I have to go, but you think about what I've said. I'll be over tomorrow."

He leaned into the car and kissed her cheek, surprising her. "Dylan, don't."

"Just a good-night kiss from a friend. Call if you need anything."

"I'll add your number to the dozens I already have," she called out to his retreating back.

"That's exactly what I'm trying to save you from," he tossed back as he climbed in his truck.

Harmony started her car and headed for home, leaving Dylan in her dust. As she drove she thought about what he'd said, about saving her.

For several years everyone had been trying to save her. They'd tried to save her before the accident—and after. They had tried to save her from the addiction. They'd tried to save her from herself. In Dawson, she'd been hoping to escape all of the people trying to save her.

What Dylan offered was a way to escape people and their good intentions. He offered a way for her to reclaim her life. What he got in return was a way to fend off the local matchmakers. It seemed like the perfect plan, yet it left her unsettled. Dylan had always unsettled her. It was his easy charm and the way he had of being completely comfortable with his life.

The flash of blue lights coming up behind her and then the wail of a siren stopped her from thinking too much about Dylan's crazy idea. She pulled over and let the ambulance pass, then she got back onto the road.

She would have gone on home but the ambulance turned up the gravel drive that led to Bill and Doris Tanner's place. Harmony followed close behind. Her heart gave a painful thud as she watched the EMTs jump from the vehicle, meet Bill in the yard and then follow him into the house.

Local volunteers were already on scene. A fire truck was parked close to the barn. Harmony stepped out of her car and watched as several men rushed out of the house for equipment. Another man led Bill outside. He saw her and shook his head.

Harmony approached, unsure but knowing someone had to be there for Bill Tanner, a man who had already lost too much.

"Mr. Tanner." She touched his arm and his face

crumpled, giving way to a few tears that streaked down his weathered face.

"Doris had a stroke. I was fixing her a hot dog and she just wouldn't move from the chair."

The volunteer moved Bill to the side as the paramedics pushed the stretcher through the front door and to the waiting ambulance. One of the men hurried to Bill's side.

"Bill, she's responding. We'll get her to Grove and then I think they might fly her to Tulsa."

"Bill, I'll drive you," Harmony said, taking hold of the older man's arm. "Should we go on to Tulsa or wait?"

"I'd wait. If they can keep her in Grove, I think they will." The volunteer smiled at her. "That's real nice of you, Miss Cross."

She nodded and old Bill Tanner gave her an odd look. "You don't mind driving me? I think my old truck will make it, but I'm a mite shaky."

"I don't mind. We're neighbors and that's what neighbors do."

They headed for her car and a truck pulled up, headlights catching them in twin beams of light. A tall figure stepped out, adjusted his cowboy hat and headed their way.

"Dylan." Harmony released a pent-up breath she didn't realize she was holding.

"What happened?" He looked from her to Bill.

"Doris had a stroke. Miss Cross was nice enough to offer me a ride." Bill's voice was shaky.

"Let me take you." Dylan nodded toward his truck.

"I can do this." Harmony insisted, but she already knew that Bill would rather go with Dylan, someone he knew and felt comfortable with.

"Miss Cross, it was nice enough of you to offer, but Dylan won't mind being up all night, sitting in a waiting room with an old man like myself."

Harmony looked from Bill Tanner to Dylan. "Do you want to drop the kids off at my house?"

"Yeah, I'll meet you at your place." Harmony nodded and watched him walk back to his truck with Bill. She stood for a moment in the yard that had been ablaze with lights from emergency vehicles. In the distance she heard the wail of the siren as the ambulance headed for Grove. The volunteers were pulling away from the house.

She got in her car and pulled down the driveway, turning toward her house. She could see Dylan's truck, already heading that way with Cash and Callie. This hadn't been in her plans when she came to Dawson, getting so involved. There were good reasons for keeping to herself. But maybe the reasons to get involved were just as good.

When she got to her place, Dylan was helping Callie and Cash out of the truck. Harmony reached for Callie's hand and Dylan followed her inside with Cash.

"You'll be okay?" Dylan asked as he settled Cash on the couch and handed over a diaper bag.

"We'll be okay." She glanced down at Callie, who didn't offer her a smile. A smile would have given her a healthy dose of confidence that she really could have used.

Dylan pulled up to the Cross Ranch the next morning. His eyes felt like sandpaper was rubbing against them and a look in the mirror confirmed that he looked as rough as he felt. He parked his truck and sat there a minute. The front door of the old farm house opened and Harmony stepped out.

She stood on the porch watching him, waiting. She would be wanting information on Doris Tanner. He opened the truck door and got out. He hoped she had a pot of coffee brewing, because he was going to need it if he planned on getting through this day.

"How is she?" Harmony sat down on one of the rocking chairs. He took the other.

"She's going to make it. They were able to keep her in Grove. Bill is still at the hospital. Fifty-two years they've been married. He said the only time they've been apart is when he served in the military."

"That's a lot of years of loving another person."

"Yeah, it is. Are the kids still sleeping?" He leaned back in the rocking chair to wait for her answer and he wished like anything he could fall asleep on that front porch with the morning breeze and the sound of cattle, probably from Cooper Creek, in the distance.

"They are. I have coffee."

"I was hoping." He sat forward in the chair planning to get up but she stopped him with a hand on his arm.

"Stay. I'll bring you a cup."

"You don't have to."

She smiled down at him and he had to admit, when she smiled, it lit up a man's world. Not that he was interested, but it felt good to know that he wasn't too far gone.

She patted his hand and her smile teased. "If we're going to have a truce and be allies, I think we might want to make it believable."

"That sounds like a plan, Harmony. I like the idea of us being allies."

"Purely platonic, right?"

"Platonic. Yes, just friends. But having each other will hopefully mean a lot less people nosing in our business."

Her hand left his and she walked inside, the screen door banging softly behind her. He leaned back in the rocking chair and closed his eyes. From inside he could hear her singing along to the radio. He pulled his hat down over his eyes.

When he woke up, the sun was full on his face and it was hot. He came awake slowly, remembering where he was and why his back hurt. It was Saturday morning and he was sitting in a wooden rocking chair on Harmony's front porch because he'd been up all night.

What had happened to that cup of coffee? He glanced at his watch and realized he'd been sleeping for a while. He started to push himself out of the chair but stopped when he heard laughter from inside. Callie said something in her high pitched, four-year-old voice. The sound of a guitar followed. Loud strumming and then soft. A moment later the strumming ended and turned into a song played by someone who had been taught by the best. Two voices, Callie's and Harmony's, sang a familiar country song.

He pushed himself up, stretching to relieve the kinks in his back. When he walked through the front door Callie looked up, her smile growing wide. Cash was stretched out on the floor pushing a toy truck. Harmony stopped playing the guitar and set it to the side.

"Don't stop on my account." He picked up the twelve-string acoustic and put it back in her hands.

"I think we're done." Harmony leaned the guitar

carefully against the table next to her. "Are you hungry?"

"You babysit *and* cook breakfast?" He plopped down on the overstuffed sofa and watched with a smile as her cheeks turned pink.

"I'm multitalented." She reached for the cane next to her. "And I can get you that cup of coffee now that you're awake."

"I definitely need it. One hour of sleep is going to make for a long day."

He started to get up but Cash drove the truck over to his feet and made a siren sound. Or something that resembled a siren. Dylan moved from the couch to the floor and the little boy scooted next to him. He had a great smile, and his mom's eyes. His blond hair would probably turn brown as he got older. For now he sucked his thumb and sometimes made it to the bathroom instead of wetting in his pants.

Katrina had insisted they start potty training early. Because she'd known she would be gone. She'd known it would all fall on Dylan, but that he'd have family to help. She'd counted on that, on the Coopers being involved in the lives of her two children.

She'd come from a crazy, mixed-up family herself and she had wanted something more for her kids. So she'd made him their guardian early on, before anyone could say she wasn't in her right mind. No one as young as Kat should lose a battle with breast cancer, Dylan thought. If he could have fought the battle for her, he would have.

Callie had found a toy truck with a horse trailer that included horses. She pushed it to his side and grinned up at him, but something was missing in that smile.

She was a smart girl, his Callie. She always seemed to know when he was lost in memories. She got lost, too, sometimes. She had nightmares and sometimes cried and hit for no reason. Dylan's mom, Angie Cooper, had recommended a psychologist who could help a child process grief.

"Breakfast," Harmony called from the kitchen. Dylan smiled down at the children. Callie pushed her truck away from him and brought back the television remote.

"Do you want to watch cartoons?"

The four-year-old nodded. Her blond hair matched her brother's but Katrina had insisted it would stay blond. Dylan kind of doubted it. He channel surfed until Callie nodded her head at a show with ponies. After giving them each a hug, he walked through the dining room to the big country kitchen.

Harmony's back was to him. Her shoulders were stiff and she was leaning on the counter. He walked up behind her and put a hand on her back. Her shoulders flinched. He rubbed her shoulders until she started to relax.

"Can you take anything for the pain?" he asked.

"Non-narcotic pain reliever. Over the counter, mostly. I drink lots of herbal tea." She moved away from his touch and turned to look at him. "It just happened, you know."

She meant her addiction. He waited, knowing she would talk about it when she was ready. Instead she shook her head. "It's getting better."

"Yeah, that's how it is with pain."

She took a biscuit out of the microwave and handed it to him. It was piled with cheese, bacon and fried eggs.

He leaned against the counter and took a bite while she poured them each a cup of coffee.

"Callie and Cash seem to be adjusting."

He nodded, following her to the dining room. "It hasn't been easy for them, moving here, where everything's different and there's no one they know from their old life."

"I'm sure it hasn't been easy for you, either. You left here a single guy on your way to a bull ride and came back, what, a year later a dad to two kids."

"Something like that. Katrina was a good mom." He pulled out a chair from the old oak table in the middle of the big room. "The kids don't—well, Cash doesn't understand. Callie gets it but she still worries that her mom will come back to the house in Texas and we won't be there."

"I'm sorry." She absently stirred her coffee.

"Yeah, well, life isn't always easy, is it, Harmony? We were pretty full of ourselves ten years ago."

She smiled at that. "*You* were full of yourself."

"And you were the princess."

"Life has a way of making us look at things a little differently." She took a sip of her coffee before continuing. "One day you're the princess and the next day your best friend is gone, your body is broken, you find yourself hooked on painkillers and…"

He put the biscuit back on the plate and took a long look at the woman sitting next to him. She didn't look broken. She still looked like a princess. He guessed he still looked like the player he'd been all of his life.

From the outside someone might see two people, whole and enjoying themselves.

If they looked a little closer, they would see the pain

in Harmony's eyes, in her expression. They would see that he was about as exhausted as a man could get. Maybe they were the best allies that ever joined forces.

"If we're going to do this, we need boundaries." She stirred her coffee some more.

"Boundaries?"

She looked up. "Dylan, I came here because I was looking for space. Not a relationship."

"Me, too. That's why we're perfect for each other. I know where you stand, you know where I stand. As long as we're helping each other, we have a good reason to tell the rest of Dawson to leave us be."

"You really think this is going to stop people from offering to help?"

"It won't stop them, but it will slow 'em down a little. Especially the matchmakers who think I need a wife."

She smiled at that. "That bad, huh?"

"Worse than bad. I think they had a list of prospects written up before I came home." He finished eating the last bite of biscuit and had to admit, she wasn't a bad cook. "What about you?"

"Me?"

"What are your plans for the future? How long are you staying in Dawson?"

She shrugged, slim shoulders under a pale blue T-shirt. She played with the handle of the coffee cup and didn't look at him.

"I don't know. I thought if I came here, I'd find the person I used to be, before life got crazy. I need time and space to put my life back together. And then maybe I'll go back and finish college. I always thought I'd be a teacher."

"Not a singer?"

She shook her head and smiled up at him. "I'm not the musician in the family. I leave that up to Clay and Lila." Her older brother and little sister. He knew that both had somewhat decent careers.

"You're good. I heard you playing."

"I'm okay, but not good. I play for myself. I hadn't played in years but since I had the accident I've picked it back up."

A screech from the living room ended the conversation, reminding him that with Cash and Callie in his life, he had no room for relationships. All of his energy went to raising the two kids in the living room.

He headed that way with Harmony following. What he found in the living room were two kids wrestling over one toy. He scooped them up in his arms and gave Harmony an apologetic smile.

"I think it's time for me to get these two home for a nap. And maybe I'll see you at church tomorrow."

"I'm not sure," she responded as she gathered up the diaper bag and followed him to the door.

He had a feeling that "not sure" meant no way would he see her in church.

Chapter Four

Harmony hadn't planned on attending church; it just happened. At some point during the long, sleepless night while pacing the living-room floor, she'd decided to give faith a second chance. She'd stood at the window watching the sky turn from inky darkness to gray to palest pink on the eastern horizon, and realized she'd been empty inside for a long time.

In the stillness of early morning she'd leaned her forehead against the cool glass of the window and thought about being fourteen again. Fourteen and knowing what she wanted out of life. Chasing calves as she helped her dad with immunizations, dozing in the green grass of the field as bees buzzed and a horse grazed nearby, her brother somewhere close playing the guitar and singing an Elvis song.

She'd known herself then. Her faith had taken her to Cooper Creek with several other members of Dawson Community Church for a late summer baptizing service.

As she'd packed her bags to come to Dawson, she had said she needed a place to be alone, without family and friends invading every quiet inch of her life. It hadn't been the complete truth. She'd come to Dawson to find joy in life again. Dawson was the place where she remembered being happiest.

She'd been hoping that coming here would help her bring the pieces of her life back together. And one of the missing pieces was the faith she'd walked away from.

Several hours after that revelation, she stood in the parking lot of the church looking up at the white building with the steeple reaching to the sky wondering what she'd been thinking. How had this been a good idea? It wasn't that easy, to fix a life. Church wasn't the bandage she could put on the last seven or eight years of mistakes and expect them to be instantly fixed.

A car door slammed, startling her. She leaned heavily on the cane that she hadn't been able to leave behind today. The pain started at the top of her spine and radiated down to her ankles. The pain of having been put back together with pins and rods.

The other late arrival was Dylan Cooper. She watched as he settled Callie on the ground and then lifted Cash from the truck. He turned to smile at her and she was struck by how his appearance calmed her nerves. His smile made her feel a little less alone. Because they were united in watching each other's backs, she decided. There was nothing more to it.

"You should keep moving unless you want to start rumors." He shifted Cash to his left hip and reached for Callie's hand. "If you're okay with that, I'm your man."

She smiled at the little girl holding tight to his right hand, then lifted her gaze to Dylan's. She didn't know what to say. She looked back at the church and then to Dylan. He winked, as if he understood.

"It's easier to walk in with someone than to walk in alone the first time back."

"I can't imagine you ever being anywhere but here, in this church. I can't imagine you ever having a crisis of faith."

"Harmony, everyone has those moments. Just because I'm a Cooper doesn't mean I bought into faith without doubts, without questions. That's one thing my parents instilled in us, though. They taught us to make our faith our own. Sometimes that means questioning."

The church bells rang. Harmony reached for Callie's free hand. Dylan was right; it was easier walking through the doors with him and the two children. It was easier being a part of a group instead of being alone. But as they moved toward the front of the church, she tried to let go of Callie's hand, to break the connection. Sitting with Dylan would be taking the charade too far. She spotted an empty space in a pew near the back, the perfect place for her. Callie held tight.

"I should sit down." Harmony eased away from Dylan and his family of three.

"Why would you do that?" Dylan let the squirming Cash down and the little boy took off as soon as his feet hit the ground. His goal was clear, he was heading for Jackson Cooper, Dylan's older brother. After hugging Jackson's wife, Maddie, and his daughter, Jade, Cash climbed the pew and landed in Angie Cooper's lap. Dylan's mom held the little boy tight, whispering in his ear and smiling as she glanced back to find Dylan.

"Sit with us." Dylan reached for her arm. "I promise, it won't hurt."

She thought it might. But with Dylan holding one arm and Callie holding tight to her hand, Harmony didn't see that she had a choice. Dylan was a strong force, like getting caught in fast-moving water. He led her to the open space next to his parents and waited as she took a seat next to his mother. Somehow Callie ended up on her lap and Dylan sat next to her.

As the music started she glanced at the man sitting next to her. The man who had once been a boy who teased her. He'd also been a friend. If she thought back far enough, they had tormented each other plenty, but they'd also laughed a lot.

Dylan was no longer a boy. He'd grown into his gangly, teenage good looks. His features were strong but lean and handsome. His skin was tanned a golden brown and his dark hair, a little on the long side, curled at his collar. With strong hands he held a child in the easiest way, but he also knew how to hold a woman in a way that she felt his strength.

Dylan Cooper was dangerous. Sitting next to him as she tried to put her life back together was dangerous.

So why in the world had she agreed to his plan? As the music continued, her mind shifted to other thoughts, ones about being lost and then found. Thoughts about being on a solid rock. Unwavering. Strong.

Strong enough to fight temptation that sometimes took her by surprise. Strong enough to fight the pain that woke her late in the night. Physical and emotional pain. Because sometimes in the dark of night she remembered Amy's face after the accident. She remembered reaching for her best friend and not finding a pulse.

She closed her eyes, needing that everlasting faith

that would get her through the coming days, weeks, months or even years. Whatever it took to get past these difficult times.

A hand reached for hers. Not Dylan's hand, Angie's. Harmony smiled up at the woman she'd known for so many years, a woman who walked with faith. Angie squeezed her hand and then patted it. No words were spoken but the gesture, the look in her eyes, said everything Harmony needed to hear.

It would get easier. Harmony wondered how many times Angie had given Dylan that same talk, the same look. Give it time, the look said. Angie Cooper understood.

The sermon ended. Toward the end she'd faded, not hearing all of the words. As had happened often in her life, her mind had focused on the words of the songs, small sermons in their own right. The words of a song could take a person to another place, reaching the innermost places of their being. She needed to know that every step she took would lead her somewhere. To a place where she would be stronger, a place where her doubts wouldn't continue to hold her hostage. She wanted to be free from this place where guilt held her chained to the recent past.

Around her people were standing, saying goodbye, discussing the price of grain and what cattle were going for this week at the stockyard. Callie had long since left Harmony's lap and had headed for Blake Cooper and his wife, Jana. Harmony remembered Jana from years ago, and the year she'd left Blake.

Their daughter, Lindsey, lifted Callie and turned to say something to Jackson's daughter, Jade. Behind the girls stood Reese Cooper, now married with a son and a baby on the way. He had lost his vision but Harmony could see that he was surviving. He had a good life with Cheyenne.

Harmony knew she needed to stand. To walk away. To go home and find a quiet place. Then a hand reached out. She looked at the man who offered it. He knew. He knew that her body ached and that standing would be so embarrassing because she was twenty-six and her body didn't work the way she wanted it to. But with her hand clasped in his, she came to her feet and no one watched, there were no whispers about her situation. He made it easy.

"Harmony, you'll come to the house for lunch," Angie Cooper said in a way that it didn't sound like an invitation but a given.

"I should go home, I…" She didn't have a good excuse. Angie knew that. Her only excuse was a selfish one. She wanted to be alone to cry. She wanted to curl up in a ball and wait for the pain to pass.

Callie came out of nowhere, a fireball of energy and happiness. Harmony smiled down at the little girl and another type of guilt hit. What she'd gone through paled in comparison to what Callie had suffered.

"Are you going to come and see the pony Jackson gave me?" Callie reached for Harmony's free hand. "He was Lindsey's pony but she's big now."

"I'm not sure. I should probably go home." She smiled down at Callie's upturned face, her blue eyes bright, her blond hair in a ponytail. "I have to check on my horse."

"Can I come with you?" Callie still had hold of her hand but it felt a lot like she was holding Harmony's heart. A person didn't walk away from a connection like that.

* * *

Dylan pulled away from a conversation with an old friend from school and moved back to Harmony's side. Callie held her hand and his mom was saying something to her. Harmony looked like a cornered barn cat, the kind that loved a bowl of milk but didn't really want to be held.

"Harmony doesn't want lunch." Callie looked up at him.

He knew Harmony was worn-out. He could see the white-knuckled grip on the cane. He knew she was looking for a way out. "I bet we can talk her into coming with us."

"I really need to check on Beau."

He shrugged off the excuse. "We can all check on the horse, and then go to Cooper Creek for lunch."

Dylan's dad, Tim Cooper, joined them and was looking from person to person, trying to catch up. "Harmony bought Terry's horse. From Bill Tanner," Dylan explained, filling his dad in.

"How's Doris? You went with Bill to the hospital, didn't you?" Jackson asked, getting in the middle of things. He had that grin on his face that meant he was up to something. Dylan couldn't say he had missed this kind of brotherly love.

"Yeah, I went with him." *What of it?* That's what he really wanted to say.

His mom gave him a curious look. "Where were the kids?"

Dylan looked at Harmony and tried to remember that they had wanted people to connect them. But it was a lot more complicated than he'd imagined. It felt like being tangled up in her life, which was the last thing he needed. He had two kids depending on him. His life now was about being their dad, or the best replica of one he could be.

Harmony needed space. He needed space.

His mom cleared her throat, reminding him he hadn't answered her question about the kids. He understood the look on her face. He was twenty-seven and everyone was waiting for him to make a mistake. He hadn't left them at the store, given them food they were allergic to or forgotten to feed them. He read to them, kept them clean and somehow managed to cook halfway decent food.

"They were with me," Harmony answered, sounding stronger than she had moments earlier. She smiled at him, then at his mom. "We were at the Mad Cow eating dinner and on my way home I saw the lights at the Tanners, so I pulled in. Dylan showed up a little after I got there."

Dylan's mom looked from Harmony to him, to Callie, and she smiled. "Well, I guess everything was taken care of, then."

"Yes, it was. And now, we should be going." Dylan wanted it to be that easy but it wasn't. He reached for Harmony's hand and felt the tremble as their fingers joined. "Hey, Jackson, would it be a problem for Maddie to drive Harmony's car on out to the ranch? I'll take her with me to check on the horse."

"Yeah, we can do that. We can take the kids, too, if you want."

A few minutes later Dylan and Harmony were alone in the truck. It was strange, the two of them sitting in the cab of his old truck with no kids in the backseat. Dylan glanced her way and saw that her eyes were closed, her mouth a firm line.

"You made it."

She nodded, then opened her eyes and smiled. "Yes, I did. I've never been good at being the center of attention."

"That's tough, being a Cross."

"Yeah, it is. That's why I've always loved it here." She pulled gum from her purse and offered him a piece. Dylan shook his head. "My dad is thinking of selling the place."

Dylan pulled onto the road and then he shot her a quick look, waiting for more information. He couldn't think that she'd be thrilled with her dad selling a place that had meant so much to their family.

"They have a ranch outside of Nashville now. He's retiring and they plan on living there full-time. They say it doesn't make sense to have two places."

"Yeah, I can see that. But he leases the land to Blake."

"He's giving Blake first opportunity to buy. I hope he'll keep it off the market until I'm ready to go home."

"You don't think you'll change your mind and want to stay in Dawson?"

She shrugged a little. "I don't know. I came here wanting a place to hide. Now it feels like I finally came home after a long journey. I didn't expect that."

"I know how you feel."

She glanced his way. "Really?"

He shifted and made the turn that would take them to her place. "A few years ago, home was suffocating me. Everyone had expectations for me. People thought they knew who or what I should be. I wanted to make my own way. I started hauling our bulls to different events. It made sense that I did it. I'm single and I don't mind being gone. But then when I ran across Katrina and she needed help, it felt like staying in Texas with her was the only option. Gage drove the truck and the bulls home and I thought I'd follow a few weeks later. I was gone a year."

"Were you..." He knew what she wanted to ask. She wanted to ask if he'd loved Katrina. But something had stopped her. They were parked in front of her barn and the Appaloosa, Beau, was grazing the short grass in the corral.

He knew that they weren't there for the horse. It was her excuse for getting away from the crowd of Coopers and taking a deep breath. He got it, because he'd needed that himself plenty of times.

She got out of the truck and he followed. They walked through the open double doors at the end of the barn, from sunlight to the shadowy interior that smelled of animals and hay. The horse walked through the stall door, whinnying a greeting but shying to the back of the stall.

"He seems to be getting used to you."

"It's only been a couple of days." She pulled a sugar cube from her pocket and held it out to the animal. Beau took a step forward, head outstretched. He brushed his mouth across her outstretched palm and took the sugar.

"I think that's progress." Dylan stepped close.

He could smell the light, floral scent of her. It was distracting in a way he hadn't expected. Especially when her arm brushed his, catching him so off guard it made his heart take a big pause.

She looked up at him, awareness flickering in the

deep blue of her eyes. Blond hair curled down her back. Harmony Cross was trouble.

Trouble because she'd always been able to unnerve him. Years ago, he'd known how to cover up his teenage insecurities with attitude and bluff, but he'd never been able to outrun what she did to him.

He could no longer act like a smart-aleck teen and loosen her horse's girth strap like in the old days. At twenty-seven what he really wanted to do was…

Well, why not? He took the step that put him firmly in her personal space, realizing that was exactly where he wanted to be at that moment. She looked as surprised as he felt, but there was no going back.

Chapter Five

They were standing in front of the stall with Beau in the corner eyeing them. It had surprised Harmony when the horse took the sugar cube. Her surprise had doubled when she looked up and saw Dylan staring at her with those hazel eyes fringed with long, dark lashes.

The air left the building, leaving behind stifling heat and buzzing flies. Her heartbeat sounded like a ticking clock in her ears. He should do something crazy now, something Dylan-ish. Jell-O should fall from the rafters or someone should jump out and spray her with a hose.

Instead he lowered his handsome face to hers. His hand slid to her back, holding her close and his lips brushed hers, light as a feather, then returning for a second, more lingering touch. His mouth on hers was firm, demanding, and yet gentle. He kissed her with the easy practice of a cowboy who knew his place in the world. She remembered the way he kissed from years ago, but this time he held her longer, easier, like he didn't want to let go.

She knew that this time when he let her go there would be no teasing words.

She knew that when he let go, everything would change. But she couldn't make herself step out of his embrace. The kiss shifted things inside her, making her feel more than her broken body, more than her broken heart.

He ended the kiss. She could hear the rushed exhalation of his breath and felt the softness of it against her ear. His forehead rested on hers and he continued to hold her close. His hands were strong, capable. She needed that strength.

"I can't say I'm sorry," he whispered as he remained where he was, holding her.

"Hmm," she murmured, not knowing what to say.

"Maybe that will clear the air."

"The air seems to be missing." She drew in a deep breath and felt a quiet breeze stir through the barn, brushing across her face. "There it is."

He grinned down at her as he took a step back. "Yes, there it is."

"We shouldn't have…"

One shoulder lifted, casual, easy. "No, maybe not, but we did. I did."

"Dylan, I can't do this."

"I know." He brushed a hand across her cheek and she wanted to close her eyes and allow herself to be the person who would turn to Dylan.

She knew she couldn't. They had a plan that would give them each space if they didn't muddle the lines and forget why they were doing this. As much as her heart responded to him, she couldn't let him be her strength. She couldn't hold on to him, thinking he would be her happiness.

She couldn't take the chance that another man would

walk away from her the minute she made a mistake, showed herself to be less than worthy. She didn't want to fail another person. She was so tired of letting people down. Most of all, herself. For five years she'd been racing through life, not thinking about the future, about how she was hurting herself and other people.

She couldn't be that person anymore. She had to want more for herself. She believed God wanted more for her.

"We should go." She had backed against the rough wood of the barn and now took a step away, toward the door. "They'll be wondering where we are."

"So we're not going to talk about this?"

She shook her head. "I think not. I'd like to pretend nothing happened and that we're still two friends just helping each other out."

"That's probably a good idea." He stepped close, offering her his arm. She took it, holding tight.

When they got to the truck she reached for the truck door. He already had it open, a big cowboy smile back on his face.

"I can pretend it, whatever *it* was, didn't happen. I can't pretend I haven't been raised to open doors for ladies."

She climbed in and smiled down at him. "You should think about getting a new truck."

"I've been thinking about it. I've had this one since I turned sixteen. Getting rid of it would be like putting down my favorite dog just because it got old." He leaned in, close. A little too close. His hazel eyes flickered with humor and she realized he had the tiniest dimple in his left cheek.

"That's very sentimental of you, but your old truck smells a lot like an old, wet dog."

"Yeah, but me and this old truck, we've made a lot of memories together."

She reached to close the door. "Go away, Dylan. I don't want to know about your memories."

He laughed as he closed the door. When he got behind the wheel of the truck, he laughed a little. "You always think the worst of me, don't you? I was talking about learning to drive, going to rodeos with Gage, those kinda memories."

"I think your memories include a pretty girl in the middle, sitting close, maybe your arm around her shoulders."

"You paint a pretty picture." He winked at her. "Annabelle Johnston. She had brown hair that smelled like strawberries."

Laughter slipped out before Harmony could stop it. "That's the Dylan Cooper I know and…"

"Love?" He flicked his gaze at her, winking again, then looked back at the road.

"Not at all. The Dylan I know and *remember*. Don't think so highly of yourself."

"I can't help it."

"No, you probably can't."

She grimaced as they bounced over a few potholes. Dylan slowed the truck down. "You okay?"

"I'm good." She pulled another piece of gum out of her purse.

"Does the gum help?"

"No, not really. I started chewing gum in rehab and it's become my new habit."

"How did it happen, Harmony?"

"What? The accident or the addiction?"

They were pulling up to the big Georgian two-story

brick home that Tim and Angie Cooper called home. It was where they'd raised their dozen children and countless foster children. Harmony had good memories of visiting here as a child. They'd gone on trail rides, had bonfires and eaten family dinners here.

Dylan stopped the truck but didn't kill the engine. He looked at her with hazel eyes that were now somber, thoughtful and nearly more than she could handle.

"I guess maybe I'm wondering about both, Harmony. But if that's too personal…"

"It isn't. It's just a long story."

"But you're okay now?"

She looked down as he closed his hand over hers. "Yes, most of the time I'm okay."

As she said it, she realized that it was becoming the truth. For the first time in a long time she really did have more good days than bad. Most of the time she did feel as if she would make it.

They entered the kitchen a few minutes later. Children attacked Dylan as they walked through the door. Callie had a picture she wanted to show him that she'd drawn with the help of Jackson's daughter, Jade. Cash grabbed his leg and Harmony noticed that the toddler didn't smell pleasant.

Dylan looked at the picture first. "Callie, that is the best pony I've ever seen."

The little girl's nose wrinkled and she frowned. "That isn't a pony, Dylan."

"It isn't?" He looked the drawing over. "Well, I'll be, you're right. That's a cat."

She frowned bigger. "It isn't a cat."

"It's a picture of Cash?"

Callie shook her head. "It's a flower."

He held the picture out and grinned big. "You're right, that is a flower and it's about the prettiest flower I've ever seen."

"You knew it was a flower," Callie insisted.

He ruffled his hand through the child's blond hair. "Yeah, I knew it was a flower. Now, I have to go change your brother and I guarantee you he doesn't smell like a flower."

"He's stinky."

"Yes, he is."

Callie ran off with Jade, the teenager that had landed on Jackson's doorstep two years earlier, claiming to be his daughter. For some reason Harmony followed Dylan from the kitchen. She knew several pairs of eyes followed her, and knew curious looks were exchanged. But it felt better to follow Dylan than to stay and answer questions about her relationship with the third to youngest Cooper.

How could she answer that her childhood tormentor and antagonist was becoming a friend she hadn't expected? How could she answer anything at all when she was still remembering the kiss they'd shared?

Cash squirmed on the changing table but he grinned big and reached for the toy truck Dylan handed him. A year brought a lot of changes in a person's life, Dylan reckoned. When he'd driven that trailer load of bulls to Texas he'd been as single as a guy could get. He'd been living his dreams and chasing after more.

Now he was pretty good at wrangling a squirmy toddler while reaching for a diaper and wipes. A year ago he'd used almost a whole tub of wipes in one changing. Nowadays he could change most diapers with less than five wipes. He claimed that as one of his victories.

Cash grinned at him and reached to knock his knuckles with the truck. "Truck."

"Yeah, buddy, you've got a truck."

As he finished up the diaper, he realized he wasn't alone. A shadow moved to his right and he knew that it was Harmony. She moved to his side, handing him the pair of shorts he'd placed on a nearby table.

"You're pretty good at that." She leaned in close and, man, she smelled so good.

"I've had a lot of practice."

He picked up the little guy and dropped the diaper in the trash can next to the changing table. Harmony was still watching them, her big blue eyes cautious, as if she didn't want to step too far into his life. He didn't blame her, not after "the kiss."

"It hasn't been easy, has it?"

"No, it hasn't," he admitted as they left the room. He slowed his pace to match hers. "I wake up sometimes still feeling like the guy that left here free and single but then I hear Cash crying from his crib or Callie at the door asking for breakfast and I'm back in my reality."

She didn't reply. He guessed in her own way she woke up to a different reality every day, too.

Callie met them in the dining room. The family was sitting down to eat and he could see that three chairs were left at the end of the table, plus a high chair for Cash. For a moment Dylan faltered and couldn't move forward. He looked around the table at his big family and he saw how much had changed the past couple years.

Changes that he guessed his family must be expecting for him, because they were seeing him as a part of a pair now. Would they start calling Harmony and him a couple? Is this how it had started for Jackson and Maddie a couple of Christmases ago? Sophie and Keeton West had fallen in love next, and Sophie now had a baby boy, as well as Keeton's daughter, Lucy. And then Reese had taken the plunge with Cheyenne. Their little boy had his own high chair between their seats and Cheyenne was pregnant with a little girl.

He glanced to the other long table in the room, because it took two long tables to seat all of the Coopers. His brother Jesse was seated with his wife, Laura. And Mia had married one of Dylan's best friends, Slade McKennon. He thought maybe Mia had loved Slade for years.

Gage had taken him by surprise. He'd never thought, not in a million years, that his angry little brother would be smiling like a cat in the cream. But he did smile as Dylan's gaze landed on his. Gage had married Layla Silver last spring.

The happiest man at the table had to be Dylan's older brother Blake. Blake's wife had returned to Dawson after ten years and she'd brought Blake's daughter, Lindsey, back. The three of them were seldom apart these days.

A lot of these changes had taken place since Dylan had been gone. He'd missed a couple of weddings, the birth of a baby. He'd missed his grandmother falling in love. Myrna Cooper wasn't at the family lunch today. She and her husband, Winston, had gone on a cruise.

Changes.

He sat down next to Callie, who had taken the seat between him and Harmony. The little girl reached for his hand and Harmony's as Tim Cooper prayed a blessing over the meal.

After the "amen," he raised his head and met his sister Heather's curious look. She'd visited him in Texas and helped him more than anyone knew. Somewhere along the way they'd gone from tormenting each other to keeping each other strong.

The only one missing from the table was Dylan's little brother Bryan. He'd gone with friends for a summer mission trip to South America and he'd stayed. He'd been gone a few years now, only coming back home for a week or two each year.

"Dylan, what do you think about that new stud horse Jackson is looking at?" Tim Cooper passed a plate of roast as he asked the question.

"I'm not sure if I like him."

Jackson cleared his throat. "Well, I do."

"You're getting old and your eyes aren't as good as they used to be." Dylan smiled as he said it. The conversation felt good. It eased the tension that had settled in his gut.

"What's wrong with him?" their oldest brother, Lucky, asked. Lucky's wife, Eva, had left the table for a minute. Soon she returned with a pitcher of tea.

"I've seen a few of his colts," Dylan explained. "I know he looks good on paper, Jackson, but the colts he's throwing aren't up to Cooper Creek standard. I'm not saying they wouldn't work cattle but I don't like the way the way they're put together. A little short in the neck and long in the body."

"Maybe we can get a good look at a couple of them?" Jackson spooned potatoes onto his plate.

"I think there's one down south of Oklahoma City."

"I'll take a drive down there one day next week."

The next thirty minutes passed this way, with conversation drifting around the table, changing frequently, sometimes midtopic.

Somehow Callie ended up in his lap, her eyes closing and her head nodding forward. He cuddled her close and watched as Harmony stood to help clear the table. She said something to Cash, her voice soft. Cash grinned and popped a bean in his mouth. Harmony was the farthest thing from broken. He wondered if she realized that about herself. He let it go. There was a sleeping kid on his lap and one in a high chair rubbing potatoes on the tray.

Harmony reappeared from the kitchen. "I should go."

"Let me walk you out." He started to stand but her hand dropped to his shoulder.

"Stay. And thank you for today. It was good to be here again."

"Call if you need anything."

A smile broke across her face. "You do the same."

And then she walked away, saying goodbye to his family as she left. Heather followed her from the room and he fought the urge to go after them, to make sure the conversation didn't turn to one that would include him and Harmony.

Callie had fallen sound asleep in his lap, though, and Cash had gone from painting with potatoes to dropping them on the floor.

"Hey, little man, that's about enough of that." He reached for a napkin and wiped off pudgy toddler hands. "I think its nap time for both of you."

From his lap Callie mumbled that she wasn't sleepy. Right, of course she wasn't. He managed to stand up.

Callie's arms went around his neck and she held tight. He moved the high-chair tray back and the sticky mess of a kid that climbed into his free arm.

"Are you heading home?" His mom walked from the kitchen, wiping her hands on a towel.

"I think so. Do you need me to do something before I go?"

She surveyed the three of them and shook her head but he saw the brief flash of concern in her eyes. "No, I think we've got it covered. Gibson called today to ask if we'd seen Harmony. She isn't answering when they call and he's worried."

Of course Harmony's dad was worried. "She's fine, Mom. I know their concerns but she hasn't slipped. You can tell them that. She just needs a little time without the whole world circling, wondering if she'll make it."

"When a parent wonders, it's different than the world wondering, Dylan."

Heat settled in his cheeks, a condition he hadn't experienced in quite a few years. "Yeah, I know. I'll have her call them."

"Are the two of you…"

He laughed at the cautious but hopeful look on her face. "It might not look like it, Mom, but Harmony and I have a lot in common."

They were both trying to make the best of the hand they'd been dealt.

His mom kissed Callie's cheek and patted his. "Of course."

Right after that he escaped. He got two kids buckled in the truck and headed back to his place, barely slowing as he passed the driveway to the Cross Ranch.

Chapter Six

Harmony awoke with a startled cry, her own. Perspiration soaked her hair and at the same time she felt cold, wretchedly cold. The dream was the same one she'd been having since the accident. A flash of light in a dark, rain-soaked night. The crash of metal. The scream. And then silence. Pain followed the dream. Or maybe pain caused the dream. Maybe the pain that shot from her back, down her left leg to her foot was the reason her sleep-fogged brain relived the accident in her dreams.

The accident had left her broken. A fractured back, shattered leg and a heart unable to cope with the guilt. She couldn't relive that night without remembering how it felt to watch her best friend slip away. She'd held Amy's hand, begging her not to go.

She'd prayed. She'd cried out. She'd pleaded. She'd yelled at God to send help.

There would be no going back to sleep now. She crawled out of bed, glancing at the clock. It was seven o'clock, Wednesday morning. She had a meeting today. There were times she told herself she didn't need the meetings. She didn't need a support group. She was clean, had been clean for months. She wasn't going to slip.

But she could. She knew that. So no matter how much she didn't want to walk through the doors of the church in Grove and say that she was an addict, she would do it. She would face the embarrassment. She would face the shame. Because she wanted to stay clean.

She owed it to Amy, to the life Amy would have had if…if Amy hadn't gone out on New Year's Eve to rescue Harmony. If a drunk driver hadn't run that stop sign. If Amy was still alive, planning her wedding, her future.

Harmony walked out the back door, breathing in the crisp, autumn air. She closed her eyes and thought back to what life had felt like years ago when she'd spent summers here. She'd known how to pray then. Now when she prayed, she felt like a fraud.

How did she get back to where she'd once been? How did she become that person again? She knew it wasn't possible. She couldn't go back.

She could go forward, the thought whispered through her mind. It gave her hope, that thought. As if God himself had whispered a promise to her.

Her cell phone rang as she walked back into the kitchen. Her mom's number and picture flashed across the front of it. She couldn't talk now. Her emotions were too raw, too close to the surface.

Today she would be going to group. But first, she had to take care of her horse.

A short time later, dressed in jeans, a T-shirt and boots, she walked out to the barn. The air smelled like autumn, drying grass and a hint of rain. In the distance cattle mooed. Somewhere a donkey brayed. And as she got closer to the barn, Beau whinnied a greeting.

The horse hurried toward the fence, eager for a sugar cube. She leaned her cane against the fence and pulled the treat out of her pocket. She held it in her flattened palm. The horse nuzzled her hand and then took the sugar. He eyed her cautiously, watching to see if she would make a sudden move. She didn't. His lips came back, velvety soft and his breath warm. Slowly she moved, brushing her fingers across his face. He snorted and took a step back but then returned for another light stroke.

He already looked better. His eyes were brighter, his body filling out. She thought maybe he'd been brokenhearted, missing his owner. Now, somehow, he knew he belonged to someone again.

"That's it, sweet boy. We'll be friends. You don't have to worry." But what about when her dad sold this place and it was time to go?

She didn't want to think about leaving, not today. She leaned close to the wood rails of the fence and Beau met her there, his face just inches from hers. She kept her hands on the rails and talked softly to the animal.

"We'll be friends, won't we, Beau? You and I, we'll heal together. We'll help each other get strong again. When I leave, you'll have to go with me."

Her thoughts turned to Doris Tanner. She'd been moved to the nursing home. Today, after her group meeting, Harmony planned on visiting her. She'd heard that Doris and Bill Tanner had lost their only child, a son, years ago in a car accident. His wife had been with him. The Tanners had raised their grandson, Terry, only to lose him in Afghanistan. A life fraught with heartache, but strong on faith.

That's what Vera had said at the Mad Cow the previous evening.

When Harmony had thought to eat alone at the local diner, but Dylan had showed up with Cash and Callie. They'd eaten together, the four of them. People had talked and smiled. That's the way it worked in a small town. News traveled fast, and people were eager to pair up any couple seen together more than twice.

During dinner, Dylan had convinced her she needed to call home. And she would, soon. Maybe today. She just needed a little space. She needed to take a step, maybe a half dozen steps, without being asked if she was okay or if she needed help.

She didn't want to hear that people were praying for her. The words felt empty right now. She had prayed. She had called out to God. It would take time, but somehow she'd work through that. But the last thing she wanted to hear was that God had a plan.

His plan shouldn't have included Amy's death.

She had been honest about that from the beginning, but people didn't want to hear that her faith was in tatters, or that she wasn't ready to not be mad at God. They wanted to tie her up in a neat little bow, the kind with *Faith* written in gold letters. Everything should work out pretty and neat, not hard-edged and angry.

People meant well, she knew. But she needed more than the pat answers about faith. She wanted someone to tell her it was okay to be angry and that God understood her anger.

If she was alone, she could yell at God. She could be mad and no one would see, or be offended by her anger.

She could wait and hope that somehow it would all make sense, and somehow she would learn to forgive herself.

She entered the barn and Beau met her there, ducking his head to come through the open door of the stall. He stuck his head over the stall door. The routine was already familiar to him. First the sugar, and then his morning ration of grain. Sometimes another sugar cube or even a carrot before she left. As she walked through the quiet, dark interior, switching on the single bulb light that hung from the ceiling, something scurried past. She shrieked and jumped back, nearly falling, but catching herself by grabbing the stall door. Pain shot through her back and her knees buckled.

"Great." She leaned for a moment against the solid wall, taking deep breaths as white-hot pain shot through her body.

The furry critter scurried past again. A kitten. Where in the world had a kitten come from? Then she saw another. It slipped out from under the second stall and joined its sibling to race through the barn into the feed room.

Harmony took a cautious step, resulting in another stab of pain up her leg.

She could do this. She would walk it off. She would focus on other thoughts, on the things around her. Sometimes it helped. Sometimes it didn't. She had to breathe and wait for the pain to subside.

She sank down on an old bench nearby, leaning against the wall, aware that the kittens were curiously stalking her feet. She closed her eyes and relied on the old trick of singing to herself. Anything to focus her mind somewhere other than the pain.

Without realizing it, she picked a song from church.

She sang quietly, opening her eyes as the pain slowly ebbed. One of the kittens had returned to its hiding place. A tiny calico, bright orange, white and black, remained. It was sitting a short distance away, cleaning its paws and occasionally stopping to look at her.

She kept singing. The horse had finished his grain and stood in the far corner of the stall, his curious gaze focused on her.

Time to go. She stood carefully, easing to her feet. As she left the barn, the kitten hurried back to his home in the empty stall at the end of the aisle.

She found her cane still leaning against the fence and made her way back to the house. As she walked up the steps, the phone in her pocket buzzed. She pulled it out and sighed. Her mom again. She started to answer but couldn't. Not yet.

The words *stubborn child* flashed through her mind. Yes, she was stubborn. Her parents had always told her she was too stubborn for her own good.

She knew she'd pushed her family away, the same way she'd pushed God away. With a child's attitude that she could do this herself.

She'd always been that child, the one wanting to prove herself. The one fighting for attention. Her brother was more talented. Her sister outshone everyone around her. Not just with her beauty, but with her heart. Lila Cross glowed from within. She had a faith that never wavered. She had talent that no one questioned.

Harmony had struggled with everything. She had struggled to figure out where she belonged in the Cross family, and she'd struggled with the feeling that she didn't belong.

A truck pulled up to the house. She waited on the

porch for Dylan to get out. In the backseat she saw Cash and Callie and waved. Callie waved back.

Dylan left the truck running and the door open. He looked as if he'd gotten less sleep than she had. But on him it looked so good. Like worn jeans and soft cotton T-shirts.

She managed a smile, then her eyes lit on his face for a long while. She saw the shadows under his hazel eyes, the dark stubble across his cheeks. He pushed his hat back a smidge and smiled at her as he walked up the steps.

"Dylan." She lifted a wary gaze and waited.

Something had brought him here this early, but she wasn't sure if she wanted to know what.

Dylan leaned against the post on the porch. "Your dad called me this morning. He asked me to check on you and to make sure you call him."

"Why would he call you?"

A flush of red bloomed under stubble that shadowed his cheeks. "I guess he heard that we've been seen together."

"And?"

"And he wanted me to know." He glanced back at the truck. "Harmony, just call him."

"Not until you tell me what he said to you."

He let out a long sigh and pulled the hat off his head to swipe a hand through his dark, unruly locks.

"He said I needed to realize that you're not ready for a relationship."

Of course her dad had said that. She could see him, trying to think of how to fix things, how to keep her from making mistakes or moving too fast. Her mom had always been the one who let her children make choices, live through the consequences. Her dad had tried to fix everything for them. She knew it came from his child-hood, from parents who hadn't really been there for him. That didn't make it any easier to deal with.

"I'm glad he warned you. I'm very aware of what I'm ready for, and I know that I'm not ready for a rela-tionship. I'm not going to drag anyone into this mess that is my life."

"It seems we are a little bit in each other's lives."

"We're friends who have each other's backs. Or at least that was the plan. Am I wrong?" She needed to sit down, and eased into the rocking chair behind her.

She wondered if he would walk away now. After her dad's phone call, he had to realize what a mess her life was in. Surely he would see that his plan wasn't going to work?

"You're not wrong." Dylan glanced at his watch. "We're friends and we're going to help each other out."

"Maybe it would be better if people didn't think we were together, though. I mean, *together*." She tried for an easy smile. An "I'm letting you off the hook" smile. "I can help you out with the kids, anytime, though."

He pushed the hat back down on his head. "That's getting a little melodramatic, don't you think?"

"No, not really. You have Cash and Callie to think about. I don't want to hurt them. Or you."

She bit down on her lip, waiting for him to answer. Watching as he shook his head, glanced back at the truck and then at her. A part of her wanted to give him an out. Another bigger part hoped he wouldn't walk away.

Dylan adjusted his hat and let out a long sigh that made him feel somewhat better. "I guess I trust you more than you trust yourself."

She smiled, and he thought she needed to smile more. "Maybe, but I also know myself better than you do."

"Listen, I have to go, but I also came by to ask you to go with me to the nursing home today. I know it would do Doris Tanner a lot of good to see you."

"I have an appointment in Grove this morning, but I plan on stopping by later."

"I'll meet you there this afternoon. Afterwards we can grill some burgers at my place."

She stood up from the rocking chair. He resisted the urge to offer a hand. He waited.

"What time will you be there?"

"About two?"

"See you then."

She followed him to his truck. She peeked in, smiling at Cash and Callie.

"Guess what I found in my barn this morning?" she asked, as she handed Cash the sippy cup he'd dropped on the floor of the truck, wiping it off before giving it to him.

"What?" Callie was always up for a guessing game. Cash already had the sippy cup in his mouth, and even though it was early, his eyes looked sleepy.

The little guy was either teething or getting a cold. Either way, it meant no sleep for everyone in the house.

"I have kittens," Harmony answered Callie. "You'll have to come over and we'll see if we can catch them."

"We already have a kitten," Callie informed her.

"Do you?" She looked from Callie to Dylan, not remembering the tabby from Doris and Bill Tanner's place.

"I won't let it in the house," Dylan explained. "I'm not crazy about cats."

"You could get it a litter box. And maybe a friend." Harmony shot Dylan a smile that was half smirk.

"Some people are allergic to cats," he informed her.

She smiled and he thought about when he'd kissed her. That shouldn't be the first thought to come to his mind when she smiled like that. He should be thinking that she looked happier now than when he first pulled up. Instead he was thinking about kissing her again. Wrong answer. Definitely wrong.

"We should go." He climbed behind the wheel and looked at the woman stepping away from his truck. "Call your dad."

"I'll call him."

She walked back to the house, her steps slow but steady. When she reached the porch she turned and waved, and he nodded in response. In the backseat Callie was talking about how cute kittens were and if her cat lived in the house, it could sleep with her.

The conversation made his insides a little itchy. A kitten in the house was the last thing he needed. Well, maybe not the last. One of those things he didn't need was back at the Cross Ranch.

Dylan wondered more than a little if Harmony would show at the nursing home. He walked through the door, just him and Callie. Cash had seemed restless and it wouldn't do anyone any good to have a sick toddler at a nursing home. Fortunately Heather had been happy to babysit. Dylan and Callie headed in the direction of Doris Tanner's room.

They made it as far as the activity room when a shout caught his attention. He led Callie through the open door and into what looked like chaos. Instead it appeared to be a slowed-down version of Zumba, and in the center of it all, Harmony Cross.

She waved from the center of the crowd. Before he could stop her, Callie raced across the room and jumped in the middle of the action. Seriously? Zumba? Dylan watched from the edge of the room as two dozen ladies moved to the music. He smiled a little and shook his head. And then someone took hold of his hand.

"Join us, handsome." The woman smiled up at him. She wore sweatpants and a T-shirt that said something about cool grandmothers. Over her white curls she wore a pink bandana that matched her outfit.

"I don't think I have the moves for this." He tried to keep his feet planted on the carpeted floor.

"Oh, honey, we aren't at all worried about moves. This is about staying fit. Come on now, let's exercise." She pulled on his hand, surprising him with her strength.

Somehow he ended up in the crowd of women, hopelessly getting his feet tangled up as he tried to keep up with the steps. He shifted right, then left, almost fell and got a little dizzy.

His gaze landed on Harmony as she moved, favoring her left leg, her right hand holding Callie's. The two turned in a circle together. Harmony's dark blond hair was pulled back with a scarf, giving him a sweet view of her profile as she leaned to speak to Callie. He nearly tripped over the lady next to him. She elbowed him in the ribs and told him to keep his eyes on his big, awkward feet.

He'd never been able to dance. He definitely couldn't do an exercise class that required rhythm and coordination, especially wearing cowboy boots. It reminded him of the time some pretty blonde had talked him into trying to line dance. That hadn't worked out too well, either.

Somehow Harmony appeared in front of him. She looked back, her lips parting in a smile. Beyond that, he could see that she'd had enough.

He took hold of her arm and she didn't complain when he led her away. Instead she leaned into him, and he slipped an arm around her waist, holding her close. Callie skipped ahead of them.

"You've got some moves, cowboy," Harmony teased him, taking the glass of water one of the nurse's aides was handing out to those who finished the exercise.

"Yes, I do."

She chugged the water, then set the glass back on the tray. As she headed for the door she turned and waved at the group of women just ending their exercise session. Several of them called out to her and asked her to join them again sometime.

"That was fun and now I'm exhausted." She limped a little as they walked down the hall. Callie managed to get between them, holding each of their hands.

"Should you…"

She shot him a look that didn't let him finish. "Do *not* ask me if I should be doing that. Please."

"Gotcha. Have you seen Doris?"

"I have. She's in physical therapy. I told her we'd catch up with her when she finished."

"How long have you been here?"

She shrugged. "I had lunch with Doris."

He didn't want to act surprised. Of course she was a good person. Of course she'd been raised to think about others. He'd known the Cross family for quite a few years and knew they were good, decent people. As kids he'd spent a lot of time with Harmony.

He'd thought he knew her back then, that teenager with attitude and fire. This new version of her was different. And he liked her. A lot.

He liked her as they sat with Doris, talking about her physical therapy regimen and how long she thought she'd be in the nursing home. He liked Harmony as they discussed Bill, and the possibility of taking a few meals over to him, making sure he ate.

He liked her when they left the facility, walking into the brisk September day. She had Callie's hand in hers, and Callie was telling her a story about Katrina. He kept a few paces behind, listening as the little girl talked about missing a mommy who had gone to heaven and wouldn't come back.

He'd always thought he could handle just about anything, but the pain of listening to Callie talking about missing her mommy, who had brushed her hair and read to her at night, that was a pain he'd never expected. He pulled his cowboy hat down low and blinked quick when Harmony flashed him a sad little smile. A lump filled his throat and he couldn't say a thing because if he did, he'd probably start to cry.

Harmony seemed to get it. She opened the door of his truck and pushed the seat forward so Callie could climb in. She said something soft and soothing to the child and promised she'd have dinner with them.

She closed the door and turned to face him. Before he could react, she cupped his cheeks with her hands.

"You are an amazing man. I just want to tell you that now, because I'm sure at some point today or this week you'll do something to make me mad and I'll forget. So right now, while I'm thinking it, I want you to know, you are my hero."

He managed to keep it together before he smiled. He hoped he looked confident, and not as torn apart as he felt on the inside. From the moment he'd stepped into Katrina's life, he'd known he was doing the right thing. When he'd stood at the cemetery holding Callie and Cash, he'd known it was right. There were times though, in the dead of night, when he was alone, that he doubted. There were a lot of times when he thought there had to be someone better than him, a hardcore cowboy who loved the open road, to be a dad to Cash and Callie.

"Thanks, Harmony." He leaned and kissed her cheek. "I think you're kind of awesome, too."

"I'm the awesome girl who spent the morning at a Narcotics Anonymous meeting. You're right, I'm everyone's hero."

He heard the pain in her voice. "Are you okay?"

"I'm an addict, Dylan. I hope someday that I can say I'm clean and sober and I have no desire to take anything that would harm my body. But today..." She pulled a coin from her pocket. "Today I can say that I'm 150 days clean."

"I think that calls for a celebration. Burgers at my place. Give me an hour. I have to go get Cash from Heather's."

"I'll be there." She started to step away but stopped. "Don't let what I said go to your head. I'm sure you'll do something to convince me I'm wrong."

He laughed and reached to open the door of his truck. "I can guarantee it."

As he drove away, he glanced in the rearview mirror and saw Callie watching from her seat. She wasn't smiling. Her blue-gray eyes were serious and studying his face.

"Callie, you okay?"

She nodded.

"You upset about something?"

She shook her head. And then a big tear rolled down her cheek, followed by another.

"Callie, kiddo, you have to talk to me."

"I want to go home with Harmony."

He didn't know what to say to that. He kind of wished he hadn't pushed it. Since he had to give her an answer, he promised they would see Harmony later, and agreed it would be nice if Harmony would brush Callie's hair. The way her mommy used to do it.

Chapter Seven

After a dinner of burgers on the grill and fries, Dylan announced bedtime. Harmony watched the process from her chair in the tiny living room of Dylan's old farmhouse. It was a comfortable house. Tiny but large enough for a man and two children. He'd explained that he picked this old house on Cooper land rather than moving in the main house because he'd wanted a place for the three of them to adjust to being a family.

As Dylan rounded up pajamas, Cash climbed onto the sofa with a fuzzy blanket and a stuffed animal that had been dearly loved from the looks of it. The little boy didn't seem to feel well. She moved from her chair to the sofa and pressed her wrist against Cash's forehead. He looked up at her, big-eyed and sweet. His blond hair was growing out from the short buzz cut. His cheeks were pink.

"You don't feel good, do you, little man?" She leaned to kiss his cheek and then sat on the couch next to him.

"He's getting a tooth," Callie said, now in a pink nightgown, as she climbed onto Harmony's lap. She had a brush in one hand and a book about a princess in the other.

"Do you think that's it?" Harmony looked from Callie to Dylan, who had just walked back into the room with a pair of superhero pajamas for Cash.

Callie nodded with the look of a kid who knew. "Grammy said so."

Harmony rubbed Cash's back and he smiled up at her. His eyes were getting heavy and he pulled the stuffed animal closer to his cheek.

"Will you brush my hair?" Callie whispered to Harmony.

"Of course I will." She was getting attached. To all three of them.

"And then will you read to me?"

Harmony looked over Callie's shoulder and peeked at the book. "I have an idea. While I brush your hair, you start telling me the story."

Across from them, Dylan settled in to the chair Harmony had abandoned. She didn't look up, didn't meet his gaze. If she looked at him, she was afraid she would lose control of emotions already stretched to the breaking point.

She stroked the brush through Callie's hair, and the little girl started telling the story of a princess who had a beautiful gown and loved that gown more than anything. Callie looked back at Harmony, causing the brush to tug a little in her hair.

"Will you put it in a ponytail?" Callie asked.

"Of course. Do you have something for me to hold it with?"

Dylan unfolded long legs and stood. "I'll get the ponytail holders."

Harmony smiled because it sounded funny coming from Dylan. Ponytail holders and a cowboy comfortable in his worn jeans and boots. He returned a minute later and handed her the holders with pink sparkly ribbons.

"Pretty." She slipped the holder around the ponytail. "I think you're ready for bed, sweetie."

"Can you tuck me in?"

Harmony nodded, and followed Callie to a bedroom with a pretty canopy bed and a crib against the opposite wall. Callie climbed into the bed, pulled the floral quilt to her chin and closed her eyes.

"Pray," the little girl whispered.

So Harmony did. And the prayer took her back to her childhood and bedtime rituals with her mother. She needed to call her mom and thank her for those moments. Moments that had made her feel so safe. She couldn't imagine missing them at four years of age. After praying, she kissed Callie's cheek, straightened the blankets and slipped from the room.

Dylan was standing at the front door looking out. He didn't turn as she walked up behind him. She rested a hand on his arm.

"You're doing a good job."

He nodded but still didn't turn to look at her. "They miss their mom."

"Of course they do, Dylan. There isn't anything you can do to change that. But you're the person they need in their lives. You love them. You keep them safe."

"Is it enough?" He pushed the door open and they walked out. The only seat on the front porch was a porch swing.

They sat down together and somehow her hand ended up in his. She didn't want for that moment to feel right.

But it did. The porch swing creaked as Dylan pushed, putting it in motion

"I'm the last person who can answer that question." She wished she had an answer. "I had parents who loved me, cherished me, and look where I ended up."

They sat there in the darkening night with the sky a deep lavender deepening to midnight-blue, a red glow tinging the western skyline. Cicadas started their nightly chorus, and somewhere in the distance coyotes howled.

"Pain pills, Harmony?" Dylan asked, not looking at her as he did.

The question came out of the blue. She didn't know what to say, not for a long minute. She was the last person who should have had an emptiness in her life. A void. His question seemed to parallel her own thoughts from moments earlier.

"I never felt like enough, Dylan. I grew up as the odd person out in this family of spectacularly beautiful people with incredible talent. I wasn't beautiful. I wasn't talented."

She wasn't their child.

Dylan squeezed her hand and shook his head, "You are beautiful."

She smiled at that. "Lila is beautiful. I'm cute. I have this too-curly hair, and eyes that are too big."

"Girls are crazy hard on themselves."

"It really isn't about looks. It's about something missing inside."

"So you partied."

"I found a way to make myself spectacular. I was insecure, alone too much of the time, and I found what I thought was a life that made me happy. I got attention for being a little bit wild." She allowed the memories to draw her into the past. "But that night, when Amy…"

"I'm sorry."

She shook her head, fighting the tears. It wasn't part of their deal, crying on his shoulder. And he wasn't nearly as sorry as Harmony was. Since the accident she had often thought that she would never forgive herself. She was working on that.

"She was driving because I couldn't. I killed my best friend."

"No, you didn't."

"Really? Tell that to her mother. Tell that to her little brother or her fiancé. Tell that to my heart."

"You didn't kill your best friend. A drunk driver killed her."

She nodded but didn't mean it. "I'm trying to believe that. I tell myself that I didn't do this really horrible thing. But then I remember and…" She shook her head. "Remembering is hard."

"I can't imagine."

"Yes, you can. You remember what it was like to lose Katrina and to look at those two little people who were suddenly depending on you to keep them safe. The difference between us is that you're doing something amazing and beautiful, and you're handling it."

"Not always with the grace you think." He smiled as he said it.

"But you're not hiding in a dark room popping pills to numb the pain."

"Is that what you did?"

"I started taking the pills for physical pain. As time went on, I started taking them to keep from dealing with the heartache, and to numb my guilt."

"No one realized?"

She shrugged. "I don't think so. I think they wanted to believe I was okay. But I wasn't. When I ran out of prescriptions, I had friends who knew how to get what I wanted. It happens so easily. It starts legally and then it traps you."

"You're going to survive this."

"Of course I am. And so are you. We'll get through it together." And then she would leave. She would go back to Nashville stronger and able to take the next step.

But nowhere in the steps to recovery did she have a plan that included Dylan Cooper. She didn't have a plan to let anyone take up that much space in her heart, not when she might fail them or hurt them.

She didn't want to let him down.

"I should go," she said. The swing was still moving, just slightly, and a breeze had come up. "I want to get home before it rains."

Dylan stopped the swing.

She escaped to the edge of the porch and looked back at him. Sitting in that swing with one arm across the top of the wood frame and a smile on his face, he looked like someone easy to love, easy to get attached to. He was handsome in a lean, cowboy way with that bright smile and honest, honey-brown eyes.

"Are you running, Harmony?" He stood, and the swing rocked with the motion.

"Maybe, but if I am, it's for the best."

Dylan didn't agree. But he should. She was making perfect sense. She should leave now, before he pulled her into his arms, chasing the restlessness from her eyes and the hurt from her heart. She wasn't a child who needed to be comforted after a bad dream, or because she missed the mother she would never see again.

She was a grown woman.

As she stepped down from the porch, she stared up at him, her hair blowing around her face and her eyes a wild, dark blue in the dusky night. Her lips were kissable.

"I should walk you to your car." He walked to the edge of the porch.

"I don't think a coyote or a bear will get me in the fifty steps it takes to get to my car, Dylan."

"No, probably not. But you never know." He grinned down at her as he took the steps and stopped at her side. "Need an arm?"

"Of course not."

"Sorry, I just thought maybe…" What had he thought? "You've had a long day."

"It has been a long day, but I'm getting stronger. I think all of the walking has helped. At home, my family was afraid to let me walk to the kitchen for a glass of tea. They were afraid to let me go to town alone."

"They wanted to help."

"I know." She stopped at her car. "But this helps. The fresh air. Having space. Sometimes a person needs space to come to terms with life."

She made eye contact with him, sending a clear message that he couldn't fail to get. She still needed space. Message received.

"I need to get inside." He opened the car door for her and she slid behind the wheel. "I'll see you soon."

"Of course."

Was that disappointment in her eyes? Or was he feeling disappointed, and it was wishful thinking on his part? It had been a good day, sharing it with her, not feeling pressured or any of the other things that had gone hand in hand with women since he'd come home.

"Call if you need anything."

She looked up at him with a soft smile. "And you call me if you need anything."

"I will." He winked and closed the door.

He walked back to the house and she headed down the drive. From his porch he watched her drive all the way home. He saw her headlights flash on the house, heard her car door and watched as lights came on inside. When he stepped through the door, Cash sat up, wiping pudgy hands across his face. And then the little guy leaned over and emptied the contents of his stomach all over the braided rug Heather had bought at some designer store.

"I didn't like that rug anyway." Dylan laughed and picked up the little boy.

Cash leaned into his shoulder, brushing his face against Dylan's shirt. "Daddy."

Dylan froze, wrapping his mind around that one word. He needed time to process a word that fit a little better than new boots. But not much. He cleared his throat and blinked back the sting behind his eyes that meant grown men do cry. "Let's see if we can get you cleaned up and find you some clean clothes."

It was going to be a long, long night. And the word *daddy* kept spinning through his mind, forcing him to think about this new life of his.

He ran water in the kitchen sink and tested to make sure it was warm. Cash cried a little as Dylan settled him in the water.

"I know, this isn't our normal bath place, is it,

kiddo. But let me get you cleaned up and I'll get you a cracker. Maybe that'll help." He remembered he'd gotten crackers when he was sick. And ginger ale. Though he couldn't be sure if that's what he should give a toddler.

His mom and dad had gone to a retreat in Missouri so he couldn't call and ask. He doubted he would have called even if they'd been home.

As he wrapped a towel around Cash, he reached for the phone and dialed Heather. She would be awake and wouldn't judge. But Heather didn't answer. Harmony did. He glanced at the phone and groaned because he had called the wrong H name.

She laughed. "I remember calls like this. The kind you make and then regret. I was usually not sober when I made them."

"I'm completely sober. And I was trying to call Heather."

"Is everything okay?"

"Not exactly. I've got a sick kid and I was trying to call Heather to see if I should give a toddler ginger ale."

"Cash?"

"Yeah. I think the rug is history."

She laughed again. He loved that laugh. He thought about telling her but Cash leaned over and lost what was left in his stomach on the kitchen floor.

"I'm not much of a baby expert, but I think ginger ale would work. But you should probably call Heather and make sure. If you need me, call."

"Thanks, I will." He ended the call and carried Cash back to the sink and the sprayer. He didn't know if it was okay, but hey, he was a guy. He stood the little boy in the sink and sprayed him off and then wrapped him in another towel and cuddled him close.

"It's going to be a long night, Cash."

Cash sobbed against his shoulder. "Daddy."

Two times in ten minutes. No, he hadn't prepared himself for that. But the little boy with arms clutching his neck wouldn't take no for an answer. As far as Cash was concerned, there wasn't another daddy in the world.

Dylan hugged his little boy.

He hadn't really been able to wrap his mind around that fact. Cash and Callie had been Katrina's kids. He'd been the guy agreeing to take them so she could have peace. But each day brought the three of them closer, making them a family. Dylan, Cash and Callie.

They were his kids. And he was their daddy. He didn't doubt that someday there would be a mom, too. But when the time came, it would be his choice, not everyone in town who thought they knew what was best for him and his two kids.

After putting a fresh diaper on Cash, Dylan sat in the recliner with the sick kid. He forgot about calling Heather. He didn't call Harmony back. He curled up with his boy and sang songs he remembered his mom singing.

Sometime during the night, after a few more episodes of sickness, he dozed off. He woke up close to dawn when Callie climbed up in the chair with them. She whispered close to his ear, "I don't feel good."

Dylan groaned and held her close. *His kids.* He smiled and told her it would be okay. The three of them dozed off again. For some crazy reason he had a dream that Harmony was there, that she'd kissed his cheek and told him he was someone special.

Were dreams supposed to smell like summer sunshine and flowers?

Chapter Eight

Harmony showed up early the next morning to check on Dylan and the kids. She'd worried about them all night. She'd thought about driving over when he called. But she hadn't. She'd sat at home telling herself that Dylan didn't need her. He didn't want a woman in his life. He wanted a woman around only to keep family and friends from matchmaking. Their relationship was a matter of convenience.

What was more, she had reminded herself, she didn't need Dylan in her life. Not really. She didn't want a man to feel as if he had to take care of her. And she didn't want to let anyone else down. Not even herself.

And yet, with all of that good advice, she'd fed her horse and headed to Dylan's. The old farmhouse was a single story, two rooms wide and several rooms deep with a porch that ran across the front. She held onto the rail as she eased herself up the steps and across the wood porch. Peeking through the window she spotted Dylan stretched out in the recliner, a kid under each arm.

The front door was unlocked so she slipped inside the

house, holding a finger to her lips when Callie awoke and saw her. Even from a distance Harmony could see that the little girl's cheeks were pink and her eyes a little glassy.

Dylan didn't move. He was sprawled out, in jeans, a T-shirt and bare feet, his hat tossed on the floor next to the chair. She stepped quietly across the room, drawn to the sweetest scene she'd ever witnessed, this man and these kids. Callie dozed back off. Cash moved restlessly and curled against Dylan's side. Harmony touched the little boy's cheek and wasn't surprised that he felt hot against her hand.

Caught off guard by the moment, Harmony kissed Dylan's cheek and told him he was sweet. She couldn't resist, not this cowboy with his dark hair in loose curls, messy from having worn that hat of his and a dark shadow of whiskers across lean, suntanned cheeks.

In his sleep he smiled and said something about her being sweet, too.

As she stepped back, Callie's eyes opened wide and her mouth formed a fearful O. The little girl scrambled out of the chair and headed for the bathroom. Harmony followed through the kitchen and dining area, which was as far as Callie could make it.

"I'm sick," Callie cried after she'd gotten sick. "I'm really sick."

"Oh, honey." Harmony held out her arms and Callie flew to them. Harmony picked her up and carried her to the bathroom. "We have to get you cleaned up."

"It's yucky."

"Yes, it is. But we'll get you clean and maybe we can find something that will make your tummy feel better."

She doubted Dylan had ginger tea. Harmony's mom

had always given them ginger tea when they'd had stomach viruses.

"I'm going to be sick again." Callie wiggled out of Harmony's arms.

Okay, Harmony could do this. She closed her eyes, remembering her own mother with a cold washcloth, pressing it to Harmony's neck and then wiping her face as she pulled back her hair. When had it all changed?

She knew, though. It had changed with wrong choices, wrong friends, and the pain of her birth mother's rejection.

She shook off the memories and reached into a cabinet for a washcloth. After running it under cold water she turned to find Callie sitting on the floor. The little girl looked up at Harmony, big blue eyes popping out of a pale face. Her bottom lip trembled and big tears rolled down her cheeks.

"I miss my mommy."

Harmony eased to the floor and pulled Callie close. She wiped her face and whispered that everything would be okay.

"I know you miss her, Callie. I'm sorry, honey."

Callie climbed into her lap. "I don't like being sick."

"I don't blame you."

They sat there that way for a long time. Harmony wanted to move. Her legs ached and her back throbbed. Certain parts of her anatomy felt a little numb from lack of circulation. But Callie had fallen asleep in her arms and it seemed like the bathroom might be a safe place to hang out with a sick child. She leaned against the tub and closed her eyes, wishing she could sleep as easily as the little girl in her arms.

Eventually she heard movement in the living room.

Cash cried and Dylan spoke softly. Then there were footsteps as Dylan walked through the kitchen.

"Callie?" He called out softly.

"In here with me."

"You?" He sounded confused.

Harmony wiggled up, having slid down a little with Callie still in her arms. Moving helped get the blood flowing again.

"Me, Harmony."

He peeked around the corner. His hair had a rim where he'd worn the hat too long. His hazel eyes still looked sleepy. Cash had his arms around Dylan's neck.

"Dylan, I think he's going to be sick."

"Why would you…" But he didn't wait. He moved fast and positioned the little boy in front of the appropriate target. And he did get sick. "Oh, man, this stinks."

"How are you feeling?" she asked Dylan.

"I never get sick."

"Of course you don't." Harmony shifted Callie. "I would get him a cool washcloth. I'm not sure why, but I figured it's better than nothing."

"I need to get them some kind of medicine."

"For the fever maybe, but for a stomach bug there isn't much you can do to help them other than ginger ale or tea."

Cash turned back around, rubbing his face on Dylan's leg and crying a little. Dylan picked him up and took her advice about the washcloth. He smiled down at Harmony but she thought the gesture didn't quite settle in his eyes.

"A guy should have to take a test for this kind of responsibility. No one should just hand it to him and tell him he can be a parent."

She started to tell him he *could* do it, but stopped herself. He didn't want to hear that he could do it. She got that. She remembered the first time they'd made her stand after surgery. Everyone had cheered her on, told her she'd be back on her feet in no time. She'd known it would take time. It wouldn't all just fall into place.

"It won't be easy." She picked words she thought he expected and words she knew to be true. "But these kids don't care if you always get it right, Dylan. They love you."

"Thanks, Harmony." He let out a long sigh and smiled down at the boy in his arms. "I'm going to put Cash down and I'll be back to help you."

"That's good, because I've been sitting here a long time and I was starting to wonder how I'd get up if you didn't wake up soon and find me."

He winked. "I wouldn't leave a good woman down."

He came back a few minutes later. She shifted Callie so he could lift her. He picked the child up and headed for the door. "Don't move, I'll be back."

She waited. She hadn't planned to, but getting up seemed overrated at the moment. When he peeked back in, he smiled and stepped into bathroom.

"I didn't expect compliance."

"Sometimes I keep the stubborn me in check."

"Good to know."

She reached for his extended hands and he pulled her to her feet, and then they stood there for a moment. It took that minute for her to feel as if she could take a step.

"You okay?"

"I'm good." She sniffed a little. "I hate to tell you this…"

"Yeah, I know, I stink."

"Sorry."

"You're not too rosy yourself."

They walked toward the kitchen and the moment eased something inside her. Even with the pain, even with the future uncertain, she could joke. She could laugh again. It almost felt like being whole.

Harmony hadn't felt that way in a long time. Even before the accident she'd been in pieces, trying to figure out how to get her life back. She'd had sober moments when she'd remembered the girl who had dreamed of being a teacher, being a wife and mom. She'd remembered thinking that someday she would come back to Dawson, because she'd been happiest here.

But addiction had always reclaimed her, making her forget that person who wanted more.

Dylan's phone buzzed. "My mom."

Harmony moved away from him. Without asking, she headed for the kitchen and the coffeepot. She washed her hands using a lot of soap and a lot of hot water before reaching for the glass carafe of the coffeemaker. Dylan followed. As she made coffee he leaned a hip against the counter and talked to his mom. He winked at Harmony as he told Angie Cooper that the kids had a stomach virus and, no, she shouldn't come over. He had it handled. And then he admitted that Harmony was there, helping.

She poured water into the coffeemaker, trying not to think about the implication of his confession to his mother. She wondered what Angie Cooper would think. Would she worry, the way mothers do, that her son might be in a relationship with the wrong person? Would she worry that Harmony might break his heart?

He ended the call. Harmony switched the coffeepot on and turned to face him. "Are we lying to people?"

His eyes narrowed. "Lying?"

"There's a fine line between helping each other and letting people think we're a couple. I really can't lie, Dylan. I've done too much of that in the past, and part of my recovery is about being honest."

"I get that." He stepped close to her and she pushed him back. "What?"

"You stink, remember? And I really can't…"

The list was long. She couldn't lie. She couldn't lose someone else. She couldn't lose herself. Why had she said anything? He waited for her to finish.

But he didn't push. "If you don't mind holding down the fort, I'll get cleaned up."

She nodded, closing her eyes as he walked away. She couldn't let herself fall in love with Dylan Cooper. But then, hadn't she always loved him? Maybe *love* was too strong a word. She'd been infatuated. She'd loved his country-boy swagger and his confidence. That wasn't really love. She'd had a crush. Love was deeper than those high-school feelings that she'd forgotten over time.

Love happened when you saw into a person's heart. Love went beyond the stolen kiss or a heart that seemed to skip beats. Love happened.

She couldn't let love happen.

Dylan walked back into the kitchen a short time later, cleaned up and ready to start the day that should have been started hours ago. Harmony was sitting at his dining-room table with a cup of coffee between her hands and her long, curly blond hair hiding her face. He poured himself a cup and joined her at the table.

She smiled up at him and he realized she'd been crying. Because of him? He'd had some crazy ideas in his life, but he was starting to see that the craziest one might have been the day he told Harmony they could help each other out.

"You okay?" He sat and watched her pretend to sip her coffee.

"I'm good, just…" She shrugged one shoulder and then looked back down into her cup of coffee.

"Man, Harmony, I'm sorry." He didn't quite know what to do with her so vulnerable. How did he help her get back to the person she used to be? "Can I help?"

She laughed a little, the kind that came at the end of a woman's tears. He knew it well. He used to try to make Katrina laugh. When everything was going wrong, he would hug her and then tease her about something crazy.

He missed her, his friend. He thought about the two little kids in his living room, growing up without her.

"We could get married," he said, then cleared his throat. "That was about the craziest thing I've ever said."

Did he have to go and make it worse by tossing out a halfway proposal to someone he hadn't known in years?

Her eyes widened, tearstained and a little puffy. Her nose was red, too. Some females just couldn't cry pretty.

"Have you lost your mind?"

"Yeah, probably."

"Why would we get married? I'm not even sure if I like you, let alone love you and want to spend my life with you."

"Okay, really, you don't have to trample my feelings that way." At least she was no longer upset. He listened for a minute, to make sure the kids were still sleeping. "It was a moment of weakness, thinking about Callie and Cash losing their mom and being stuck with me. What in the world was I thinking, Harmony? I'm twenty-seven, and a year ago, having a couple of kids was the last thing on my mind."

"I never thought I'd be the girl fresh out of rehab. Life happens, it takes us by surprise, and then we find out who we really are."

"I'd like to think I'm a good enough person to do this."

She reached across the table and he took her hand in his. When she smiled, it took him by surprise. There was a flash of the old Harmony in that smile, the cowgirl who had acted as if she could take on the whole world.

He remembered her on a horse after the last barrel and heading down the home stretch, hair flying and a happy smile on her face. She'd won more than she'd lost. He'd always thought that was Harmony Cross, not the girl in Nashville living a crazy lifestyle.

Her hand squeezed his and it yanked him back to the present, and to those dark blue eyes that were studying his face.

"You're more than good enough, Dylan. You love those kids, and that is going to make up for everything you think you can't do."

"I hope you're right."

"I am." She smiled with confidence, in him.

In that moment, looking at her the way she was now, the grown-up version of the girl he'd kissed once on a dare, he thought maybe he *hadn't* been kidding when he asked her to marry him. He had to figure out his new life as a dad. She had a lot to get through in her life. Neither of them needed complications.

A few minutes later, a truck rumbled up the driveway. He heard it coming, then heard a trailer rattle to a stop. He walked to the front door just as Jackson walked up the steps whistling a country song and looking like a guy who had everything in his life worked out.

Dylan pushed the door open and Jackson grinned and walked inside. "Is that Harmony's car out front?"

"You know it is."

"Then you two are serious and not just playing everyone? Because I would have bet the farm on this all being subterfuge."

What in the world was he supposed to say to that? Dylan stared at his older brother, just long enough to look guilty. Finally he got it together. "I didn't know you knew the word *subterfuge* or how to use it in a sentence."

"Funny, but you know what I mean. You. Harmony. Pretending to like each other so everyone else will leave you alone. In your case, no one tries to fix you up with the perfect woman. And she gets to relax a little without everyone trying to fix her."

"I'm not sure…"

Jackson laughed, then quieted when he saw Callie and Cash sleeping on opposite ends of the couch. "What's wrong with the kids?"

"Stomach virus."

"Need anything?" Jackson whispered as he headed for the kitchen.

No, Dylan thought, he and his fake girlfriend were

handling things just fine. But instead he said, "No, I've got it covered."

"Hey, Harmony," Jackson said as he headed for the coffee. "I hope you made the coffee. Dylan can't even boil water."

"I can boil water *and* cook." Dylan shot his brother a warning look. Jackson could get under a guy's skin, even when he was being the most supportive member of the family.

"I'll take your word for it." Jackson stood in the kitchen holding a cup of coffee and looking from Harmony to Dylan and back to Harmony, before grinning like the cat with a cornered mouse. "You two should think about this."

"Think about what?" Dylan brushed a hand through still damp hair.

"Don't get all testy."

Harmony started to stand. "I should go."

"Sit down." Jackson said, still smiling but no longer joking. "I'm on your side. I've been watching the two of you and it doesn't take a genius to figure out that you all—" he pointed to Dylan and then to Harmony "—aren't a couple. Well, maybe a couple of fools. And really, I think what you're doing is smart. Why not help each other out and get a break from all of the people wanting to fix your lives? Smart."

Harmony sat in stunned silence. Dylan cleared his throat. He looked at her and hoped she'd relax and breathe. "We're two people helping each other out, Jackson. Isn't that what friends do? I don't remember telling anyone we're a couple."

Jackson set his cup in the sink. "No, I guess you haven't really said that, but you've let people think it."

"No, we've let people know that we don't need help because we're helping each other."

"Right. Of course. And it's good to know you're helpful, because I need your help loading some cattle to take to town. And tomorrow I need your help moving the hay we baled last week."

"I've got two sick kids. Don't you think Gage can help?"

"Gage took Layla to Eureka Springs for a few days."

"We need to get Bryan back in the country."

"Sorry, our little brother called last night and said he's staying longer. But he's coming home for Thanksgiving and Christmas." Jackson stepped away from the counter. "If you can't help, I'll see if I can round Blake up."

"No, he can help. I can watch the kids." When Harmony spoke, Dylan shot her a look.

"Harmony, helping each other out doesn't include babysitting."

"No, it doesn't, but I'd like to. If there's a problem, I'll call you."

"Are you sure you're…"

She pushed herself to her feet. "Don't ask me if I'm up to it. You know that I am."

"I know you are." He stepped close, just a foot between them. He'd been wrong, she didn't smell at all bad. She smelled like springtime. His gaze caught on her loose, blond curls. He wanted to twist his finger around one of those curls.

Jackson fortunately cleared his throat. "We should be going then. The sooner we go, the sooner we get back."

"Are you sure?" Dylan asked again as he backed away from temptation.

She smiled a little. "Of course I am."

He didn't kiss her goodbye, even though he really wanted to. A kiss goodbye would have given Jackson enough ammunition for a year. Instead he slid a hand down her arm and stepped away, following his older brother out the front door.

When they were in the truck and driving down the road, Jackson shot him a disgusted look. "Are you twenty-seven or seventeen?"

"Shut up."

Jackson chuckled. "Remember when I dared you to kiss her?"

"Yeah, I remember."

"She was a wild thing back then."

"Yes, she was." Dylan watched farmland flash by the window. They were heading for a hundred acres a few miles from the main Cooper Creek ranch. "Do you have a point?"

"Not really, just thinking that she's grown up a lot. She's gone through some stuff."

"Yes, she has." Dylan took off his hat and brushed a hand through his hair. "Jackson, if you have something to say..."

"I'm not sure what I want to say."

"That's a first." Dylan laughed. "Look, it isn't anything. It's just a friendship."

"Right. Of course it is." Jackson slid him a knowing look. "Maddie was helping me with Jade. Sophie helped Keeton with Lucy because they were friends. Jesse helped Laura with Abigail because she needed a friend. Need I go on?"

"No, I think you've made your point."

"Gage helped Layla with Brandon."

"You can stop talking now."

Jackson slowed the truck for the sharp right turn. In the rearview mirror Dylan watched Jackson's dog lean with the movement of the truck and then he barked at cars driving past them.

"We Coopers are a helpful bunch," Jackson continued.

"Yes, we are. It's the way we were raised."

"And we love nothing more than family."

Dylan sighed, a way to let Jackson know he was tired of the conversation.

Jackson didn't stop, though. "I'm just saying, little brother, that you've got history with this woman, and she has history she's trying to get past."

"Have you noticed I'm taller than you, so maybe stop with the little-brother label?"

"Just an inch or two taller and I'm quite a bit older." Jackson pulled the trailer around and backed up to the gate. "Get out and open the gate."

"When is it going to be your turn to open the gate?"

"When you're not around to do it."

Dylan swung the gate open and Jackson backed the trailer to the opening. Dylan moved cattle panels to block the space between fence and trailer so they didn't have any cattle escape.

Jackson joined him a moment later. "I brought the gray gelding for you."

"Thanks."

Jackson laughed and Dylan gave him a look he couldn't misinterpret. Jackson knew he didn't like riding the gray gelding. Every time a guy rode that horse, it took fifteen minutes to convince the animal he'd been broke for years. The gelding started every ride off like he was still green. He'd bunny hop, walk stiff-legged like he meant to throw a guy, toss his head and in general act like a colt. Eventually he'd settle down and do his job, though.

"You're welcome." Jackson grinned big and adjusted his hat to block the sun.

It took them less than thirty minutes to bring in the steers that they had to load. The dog did the running, keeping up with any animal that tried to cut from the herd. True to nature, the gray gelding had given Dylan a bone-jarring ride the first fifteen minutes. As they moved steadily toward the round pen and the trailer, the horse had settled into an easy trot, his ears pricked forward, his attention focused on the job.

Dylan's attention was anywhere but the job. His mind had shifted from cattle to Harmony and the look on her face when he'd suggested getting married. That had been just about the silliest notion ever. Settling down wasn't on his radar. He'd never met a woman who made him think about taking the walk to the altar.

Harmony deserved more than his halfhearted proposal. He'd tell her that later.

Something caught his eye. It darted, moving fast. A rabbit. It raced past his horse and the dog turned, thinking he might chase the rodent. The gelding took a wild lunge to the left and gave a mighty buck that sent Dylan flying off his back, hitting the ground hard.

As he tried to suck oxygen into his lungs, he heard Jackson laugh. Dylan eased into a sitting position, glaring at his brother.

"I'm selling that horse," he growled at Jackson as he closed the gate of the round pen, enclosing the cattle that milled and avoided the open trailer.

"Need help getting up?"

"No, I don't need help." He breathed deep, catching his breath at the sharp pain in his side. "I really don't like that horse."

"You shouldn't have been daydreaming. You're better than that."

"Thanks, I know that." Dylan pushed himself to his feet. He hadn't been thrown in years, and it didn't feel good to his body or his ego. "I wasn't daydreaming."

"You were back at your house sitting at a kitchen table wondering if Harmony is the love of your life."

"I've never wanted to hit you the way I want to hit you right now." He took off his hat, straightened the brim and dusted off his pants before grabbing the reins of the horse that had politely waited for him to get off the ground.

"Violence, the first sign of love. Do you know how many times a brother of ours has threatened to hit me in the last couple of years?" Jackson swung down off his horse and gave the dog a command. The blue heeler finished the job of loading the cattle and Jackson stepped inside the stock trailer to close a divider that would keep the cattle in the front portion and leave room for the horses at the rear of the trailer.

Dylan loaded his horse and limped to the front of the truck, ignoring Jackson's questions about his health. No, he didn't need a doctor. And no, he wasn't in love with Harmony Cross.

"End of story," he muttered as he climbed in the truck. He leaned back and pulled his hat down low over his eyes, blocking out the sun—and the smug face of his brother.

Chapter Nine

Harmony cleaned Dylan's kitchen after he left with Jackson. Cash woke up first, toddling into the room, his thumb in his mouth. She offered him crackers and tea. He sat in the chair and nibbled the crackers and then sipped from the teacup.

She didn't know what else to do for him, and the only person she could call, her mom, was hundreds of miles away in Nashville. If she did call, what would she say to Olivia Cross? She remembered her parting words and cringed.

Rather than calling, she sat at the kitchen table with Cash in her lap and swiped away a few stray tears that trickled down her cheeks. She shouldn't have blamed her parents. Her heart ached at the memory, then she buried it, instead choosing to hug the sleepy little boy curled against her shoulder.

"Harmony, are you crying?" Callie walked through the door from the living room dragging a child-size quilt and a teddy bear.

Harmony smiled and shook her head. "No, sweetie, I'm fine. I made tea that I think will help you."

"I don't like tea."

"This is a different kind of tea. It tastes like ginger and cinnamon and apple. Will you take a few sips for me?"

Against her shoulder, Cash nodded. She smiled down at the little boy. She wondered if he remembered his mommy. She knew that Callie did. The little girl had told her earlier that her own mommy used to have blond hair before she got sick. The child's memory had left a lump in Harmony's throat.

Sometimes she thought she remembered her own mother. The memories weren't pleasant. They were of a woman who always looked too thin, who never seemed warm and loving. She didn't want to be a replica of Olivia Cross's sister, Patricia. Her real mother.

"Let's get your tea and we'll go sit in the living room together." She put Cash on the ground. "Callie, can you take your brother to the sofa?"

Callie nodded, took Cash by the hand and the two tottered off together, the quilt dragging along behind them.

Harmony fixed a second cup of tea and as she did, she dialed a familiar number. When her mom answered, Harmony sobbed.

"Harmony, honey, are you okay?"

She sniffled and brushed away the tears. "I'm good, Mom. I just…" Where did she start? "I'm sorry. I'm sorry for letting you down. I'm sorry for the mess I've made of my life. Most of all, I'm sorry for what I said to you. I need time, but not distance from my family."

Olivia Cross was silent for a moment, and Harmony wondered if it was too late for apologies. She waited, holding her breath as she stirred honey into the cup, adding an ice cube to cool the liquid.

"Harmony, I love you. You are my daughter in every sense of the word. My sister might have given birth to you, but you are my flesh and blood. Mine. We just want you happy again."

"I'm working on that. Coming here to Dawson was the right decision. Probably one of the first *right* decisions I've made in a long time."

"Harmony, can I have soup?" Callie stood behind her, still holding the blanket. From the dirty edges, Harmony thought the child must find a lot of security in the patches of cloth sewn together.

"Of course you can."

On the other end of the phone her mother cleared her throat. "Who is that?"

"Dylan Cooper's daughter," she said, looking down at Callie.

"I see."

No, her mother didn't see. "I'm helping him with the children."

More silence and Harmony couldn't explain, not with Callie standing by the table watching her. "Mom, I should go. I'll call you soon. But I wanted you to know that I'm doing really well here."

"I knew you would. Harmony, your dad has some information for you."

Harmony had found chicken noodle soup in the cabinet and she opened a can while she listened.

"My sister." Olivia Cross's voice softened. "Your mother is in Missouri. We're trying to find her exact location. If you want to see her."

Did she want to find the woman that had given birth

to her? It wasn't the first lead over the years. In the past she had tried to find Patricia Duncan without telling her parents. Since the accident and everything that followed, Olivia and Gibson Cross had offered their help.

They thought maybe finding Patricia would help her fill the empty spaces in her life.

"I'm not sure." Harmony set the pan on the stove to heat. "Let me think about it."

"Okay. If you want, I could go with you."

Harmony smiled at the offer. "Thank you, Mom."

The call ended. Callie had decided to sit on the floor. She had her blanket close to her face and her eyes looked sleepy again. "I don't feel good."

"I know you don't. Can I carry you to the table?" Harmony held out her arms and Callie allowed herself to be picked up. It was a short distance to the table. Harmony held tight and thought about not falling, not failing.

There were people in her life counting on her. She had to count on herself, too. She eased Callie into a chair and went back to the stove for the soup that had started to simmer. As she poured it into two bowls the front door opened. She carried a bowl of soup to Callie.

Dylan walked into the kitchen. No, he limped. She let her gaze slide from his face to the clothes now spotted with dirt and grass stains.

"What happened to you?"

He gimped to the table and pulled out a chair to sit. "Jackson and that half-wild horse he likes to put me on happened to me."

"Do you need a…"

"Doctor? No, thanks, I'm fine. It isn't the first time I've been thrown."

She smiled. "I wasn't going to say doctor. I thought maybe you'd like another shower. You stink."

As she pulled another can of soup out of the cabinet, she looked back at him and saw the flash of a grin. He shook his head and leaned to say something to Callie. Callie laughed at whatever he whispered in her ear.

"No fair, telling secrets," Harmony warned. "Do you want soup?"

"Soup sounds great. Did you do okay? I mean…" Dylan's cheeks turned a light shade of red.

"We were just fine. They slept most of the time that you were gone."

"I think I could use a nap, too." Dylan yawned and Callie did the same. He pulled her into his lap and she settled her blond head against his shoulder.

Harmony turned away from the sight and concentrated on the soup. She waited until it reached a simmer and then she filled a third bowl. After placing the soup in front of Dylan she reached for her purse and then stood awkwardly, not knowing what to say.

"Going somewhere?" Dylan asked as he crunched crackers into his soup.

His eyelashes were long and dark. His hazel eyes were full of questions. She couldn't stay. Not here, with him, with Callie and Cash. She'd never planned this, the attachment she felt to the three of them. Down the road she saw certain heartbreak, and she knew she couldn't handle it.

"I should go. I have to buy cat food and I need milk."

"Let me walk you out." Dylan pushed back from the table and settled Callie in the empty chair next to his.

"Your soup will get cold."

"I can reheat it in the microwave. I'm going to walk you out."

He didn't take no for an answer, of course. Harmony kissed Callie's cheek and checked on Cash before walking out the front door with Dylan's hand on her arm, strong and supportive.

"You're good with them. Thank you."

"I didn't mind. They're sweet." She stopped to rest after making it down the steps of the porch. Dylan stood next to her, studying her face, making her want to know what he planned on saying so she could prepare herself.

"You'll make a good mom someday."

His words took her by surprise. She hadn't thought about it, about being a mom, anyone's mom. After all, she was her mother's daughter. Her mistakes were proof that DNA mattered more than a loving environment. She had become Patricia Duncan. And Patricia Duncan had abandoned her small child in a parking lot in Arkansas with a note that someone should contact Gibson Cross.

Sometimes she thought she remembered that day. There were times, late at night, that she would wake in a panic, thinking about being alone, being afraid.

They reached her car and Dylan still held her arm, his hand strong but gentle. She looked up into those steadfast hazel eyes and wished she could be a better person, the type of person a man like Dylan Cooper would love. He brushed hair back from her face and his hand remained.

"Dylan, I have to go."

"Let me do this." He leaned a little and she felt her heart catch at his meaning. His hand moved to the back of her neck, warm and secure.

"No." She pulled away, but her heart raced ahead of her, wanting what she knew was wrong for both of them. No relationships, she repeated to herself. No letting anyone else down. Not Callie or Cash. Especially not Dylan.

Dylan had stumbled into worse things in his life than what he felt at that moment for Harmony Cross. He'd wanted to kiss her years ago when Jackson dared him. But this felt like a tumble, a straight-out falling down, worse than being bucked off of a horse. Harmony had been in his arms, and then she was gone, backing away, her eyes wide and maybe a little fearful.

And he still wanted to pull her close and kiss her. He wanted to tell her he'd been thinking a lot that this was a mistake, this helping-each-other-out business. He wanted to tell her it was the worst thing. And holding her was the worst thing. Because how in the world could he focus on the two kids in the house when Harmony Cross had the most kissable mouth of any woman he'd ever met? Every time he got around her, he wanted to hold her close. For a real long time.

He wanted to help her. He wanted to see her strong. He wanted her to have faith in God, and in herself.

And all of that added up to one big bundle of trouble, because Harmony didn't believe in herself and she sure wasn't going to let anyone else believe in her. But he could still see in her the girl he used to know, the one that acted as if she could not only overcome mountains, but bulldoze her way right through them.

"Dylan." She sighed a little and he looked down at her.

"Harmony." He grinned as he said it, hoping to chase away the stormy gray in her blue eyes.

"Don't. Please don't make this complicated. I love Callie and Cash, and I want to keep helping you with them."

He winked. "Just them?"

"What?"

"You don't love me, too? Not even just a little?"

"I don't love you. I tolerate you and I think you love yourself a lot." Her smile had reappeared, and he was okay throwing himself under the bus to get that reaction from her. "I'm not ready for anything other than friendship."

"I know." He kissed her cheek. "And I'm sorry for pushing. We're not so different, you and I."

She laughed softly at that. "Yes, we are. You rescue people. I hurt them."

He didn't ask her to list who she had hurt. It wasn't an imaginary list, he knew that. He knew if he asked, it would bring back memories she'd probably already faced at least once today. He could see the guilt she felt. It flooded her face with emotion and the smile she'd worn moments ago disappeared.

"You're doing a good job of rescuing me and the two kids in that house." It seemed like a good idea, to remind her that she had done some pretty decent things.

"They're easy to help, Dylan."

"Yeah, they are. I don't know what I'd do without them." He remembered last night. "Cash called me Daddy last night. Man, that is a hard one to wrap my mind around. There are steps to being someone's daddy. A wife, having kids, all of the ways it usually happens."

Moisture gathered in her eyes. She reached for his hand, squeezing. "You are their daddy, though."

"I guess I am."

"Speaking of two kids, you should get back in to them and your cold soup."

"Ah, escaping. Very good."

"Yes, I have to, because I might say something that we both know would be wrong. As sweet as you are, it would be wrong. I have to put some distance between us. Maybe a few days' worth."

He opened her car door and even though he didn't agree with what she'd said about distance, he did. After walking back in the house and being confronted with two kids that were still sick, he knew he had to get his focus back where it belonged. Cash woke up, still sick. Callie crawled up in Dylan's recliner and fell asleep.

He was a dad. He guessed those two kids had rescued him as much as he'd rescued them. Because of Cash and Callie, he was a better person. He'd been forced to grow up, to make decisions he might not have made without them.

When his mom showed up it was close to evening. He'd fallen asleep sitting in the rocking chair and woke up when the door opened. He started to stand but a sharp pain in his ribs took his breath.

"Don't tell me you're sick, too?" Angie Cooper set her purse down and surveyed the scene in the living room.

Cash was groggy but awake. Dylan had placed a bucket near the sofa, just in case. Callie was awake, still in his recliner and she had a princess cartoon on TV. Dylan pushed himself to his feet but the pain in his side was a definite reminder that he'd gotten thrown from a horse hours earlier.

"I'm not sick." He winced as he took a step. "Can I get you a cup of coffee or tea?"

"No, I brought dinner for you. Is Harmony still here?"

He glanced around the room. "Why would Harmony be here?"

"Jackson said she was helping with the kids. I would have come over sooner if I'd known you were alone."

"Mom, I have it covered. I've been taking care of these kids for a year now."

"I know you have. But you're home. Why in the world are you so determined to do it all on your own?"

"Because this is my life now, and I have to adjust to being a single dad who raises two kids. My kids." He looked from Cash to Callie.

"I'm proud of you." His mom patted his arm but she didn't do more, and he was glad. He sure didn't want to cry on his mom's shoulder. Not today.

"Thanks, Mom." He headed for the kitchen with the basket of food she'd handed him. "What's for dinner?"

He walked gingerly, rubbing his side as he went.

"I think a trip to the ER for you," his mom called out from the living room. "Homemade vegetable soup for my grandchildren."

He stepped back into the living room. "What about the ER?"

"You might want to get those cracked ribs taped up?" She smiled as she pulled Cash onto her lap. Callie left the recliner for Angie's lap as well.

"My ribs are fine."

"I've been around long enough to know when one of my boys needs a trip to the emergency room, Dylan. You can't let things go. You have kids to think about." She kissed the top of Cash's head and smiled up at Dylan.

"You win."

She smiled at that. "I always do."

As he drove toward Grove, Dylan wondered if he would ever win again. There were things he'd like to win, he thought. At the top of the list, for whatever crazy reason, was Harmony's trust.

Just her trust, he told himself. Trust meant she would have to share the heartache she was covering up. She would have to share the pain that lingered in her blue eyes.

He knew it would take time, but he was a pretty patient guy.

Chapter Ten

It took Harmony two days to get over the stomach virus she caught from Cash and Callie. For those two days she gladly let Dylan feed her horse. She tried not to be upset when he stopped in to tell her he'd gotten a halter on the animal. Yes, it was all about being stubborn, but she'd wanted to be the one. Dylan doing it meant that he didn't think she could.

With the virus behind her, on Saturday she headed to town and the Mad Cow. As she got closer to the Tanner place she hit her turn signal and pulled up the drive. Several shirts and a couple of pairs of bib overalls fluttered on a line that stretched across the yard, hung between two rusted poles. Bill Tanner was sitting on the edge of the porch, looking even thinner than the last time Harmony had seen him.

She stepped out of her car and Bill looked up, adjusting his ball cap and half smiling at her. "Hi, Bill."

"Miss Cross."

She made her way across the lawn, stepping carefully through overgrown grass. "You can call me Harmony."

"I reckon."

"How is Doris?" Harmony sat on the step just a few feet from the old farmer.

He let out a long sigh and shook his head. "I don't guess she's doing too good. It's hard to see her like that."

"I bet it is."

"I went two days ago. I guess her sister is coming up from Dallas to have a look at her."

Alone. Doris Tanner was alone. Harmony thought about the great circle of friends and family that had surrounded her after the accident. "Bill, let's go have lunch at the Mad Cow and then we can go visit Doris."

"You don't need to do that."

"But I want to." Harmony stood and she held a hand out to Bill. "Dylan said you're planning a trip to the beach. We need to get Doris better so she can have that trip."

Bill took her hand and stood. "If I go to town with you, you'd better drive like you've got some sense."

"Of course I will."

A few minutes later they pulled through the one stop sign in the town of Dawson. The feed store had a display of fall items. Straw bales, corn stalks and mums of all colors. Harmony would have to make a trip back to town in the old pickup her dad left in the barn. If she was staying in town for a few weeks, fall decorations would be nice.

She pulled in to the gravel parking lot of the Mad Cow Café. It was a busy Saturday in Dawson. She parked next to a familiar truck.

"Looks like Dylan is here," Bill offered as he got out. "Guess you two are pretty serious?"

Harmony opened her mouth and then closed it, because she didn't want to look like a fish gasping for oxygen. "Well, no, we're just friends."

"Not the rumor I heard." Bill closed the car door and was already heading across the parking lot when Harmony caught up with him.

"Well, you know how rumors are, Bill."

"Yep. They usually have a smidge of truth to 'em."

The smile took her by surprise. Bill's and her own. He chuckled a little and opened the door of the diner for her. She never would have guessed this friendship, the one with Bill Tanner.

Just like she never would have expected how much she missed seeing Dylan and the kids. But she had missed them. So much that her heart did a little leap when she spotted them in the Mad Cow. Callie called out, jumping from her chair and hurrying toward Harmony, a big smile and arms ready for a hug. Harmony leaned to hug the child, holding her tight for a moment and then kissing the top of her head.

"You're better?" Callie asked as her hand tugged on Harmony's.

"I'm better. Thank you for the chicken soup."

"Grammy made it."

Grammy meaning Angie Cooper, a woman ready to love all the children placed in her life. "Well, it was very good."

"We're having chicken strips." Callie led her to the table. "And Dylan cracked a rib because he can't ride a horse."

They always had chicken strips. But the cracked rib was news to her. She remembered that he'd gotten thrown when he went to help Jackson. She shot him a look and he reddened just a little.

"You cracked a rib?"

"Two, but I'm fine."

Bill had already taken a seat at the table. He grinned up at her and winked. "Like I was saying."

"Bill," she warned in a quiet voice.

The older man laughed and reached for a menu. Harmony met Dylan's easy smile. He winked and indicated she should take the seat next to his. She didn't. Instead she pulled the chair out for Callie and took a seat next to Bill.

"Bill and I are going to see Doris," Harmony told Dylan as she looked over the menu a waitress handed her. Harmony smiled up at the woman she hadn't seen before. And then she turned to Dylan again. "Where's Breezy?"

He shrugged. "She left. Something about finding more family. A brother, maybe her dad."

"Wouldn't it be Mia's dad and brother, too?"

"No, they had different dads, she and Mia did."

"When will she be back?"

He shook his head. "She probably won't."

Harmony hadn't known Breezy Hernandez very well, but she'd liked the free-spirited sister of Mia Cooper McKennon. She smiled up at the new waitress, who had reappeared with ice water and hot tea. Harmony ordered and handed the menu back to the waitress.

And then there was nothing but time as they waited for their food. Time to look at Dylan. Or avoid looking at him. Time to think about his impulsive proposal days earlier.

"I'm planning a birthday party for Cash," Dylan said.

"When?" She smiled at the little boy in his high chair, ketchup all over his mouth as he finished eating his French fries. Cash grinned back at her, a big smile that sparkled in his blue eyes.

"Two weeks. You'll be here, won't you?"

She nodded, because yes, she would stay. It wouldn't be a birthday Cash remembered, but it was an important birthday. He was turning two. He had a new home, a new life. Even as little as he was, it mattered.

"Yes, I'll be here." She smiled up at the waitress who appeared with their food.

"What are you planning to do with that horse when you head on back to Nashville?" Bill asked as he poured ketchup over his fries.

"I'll take him with me."

Bill nodded at the answer and picked up the burger he'd also smothered with ketchup. Bill liked ketchup.

Suddenly the day seemed normal. Harmony finished her lunch and held on to that feeling. Normal. She was just another person having lunch at the Mad Cow. She laughed at Cash's silliness as he bulldozed a chicken strip through ketchup, and she answered Bill Tanner's questions about Beau and how the horse was getting along. She invited him to visit.

They finished eating and left. Callie held her hand and asked if she could ride with Harmony to the nursing home. Bill somehow ended up in the truck with Dylan. It all made sense. It all felt right.

Harmony started her car with Callie buckled in her booster seat in the back. She smiled at the little girl and then headed out, still thinking about being normal and having a life that included these people.

But it didn't last. Instead grief sneaked up on her. By the time she reached the nursing home, it had her in its grips. It happened that way sometimes. She could be smiling and laughing, thinking maybe today would be the day when she would forget.

But she couldn't forget. Not a best friend. Not a moment that changed everything for so many people.

She sat in her car for a long time after parking at the nursing home. Callie had unbuckled herself and crawled over the seat. Her little arms wrapped around Harmony's neck, and she leaned in close, smelling like soap and chicken.

"Are you sad?" Callie asked, leaning close.

Harmony smiled up at the little girl and nodded, but she didn't form the words.

Callie kissed her cheek. "Sometimes I get sad, too. I miss my mommy. Do you miss your mommy?"

Harmony sniffled and smiled, her hand going to Callie's sweet face. "You are precious, Callie. And yes, sometimes I miss my mom, too. But she's in Nashville." And Harmony would see her again.

Harmony's grief was for Amy.

"Can I see her in Nashville?" Callie whispered close to Harmony's ear as the car door opened and Dylan stood in the opening, peering down, his eyes narrowed as he studied her face.

"Maybe someday she'll come here and you can meet her," Harmony offered the child.

"Okay." Callie scrambled over her lap and out of the car. The little girl hurried to the sidewalk where Bill waited.

"What's up?" Dylan held Cash's hand and the little boy was tugging, trying to move away. Dylan held him tight.

"Nothing. I'm good."

"What was it you said about needing to be honest?"

Dylan gave Cash a warning look. "Buddy, stop pulling on my hand."

Cash stopped. Harmony grabbed her purse and got out of the car, forcing Dylan to take a step back. She closed the door and locked it, then faced the man standing behind her, waiting for her answer.

"Everything seemed so normal back at the Mad Cow," she explained. "Everything seemed right. And then I remembered that Amy is gone and I'm the reason why. How can I have normal moments, feel happy, have lunch with a friend and get hugged by a little girl like Callie, when…"

Dylan's right arm pulled her close to his side and he leaned down, his lips brushing close to her ear. "Stop. Give yourself a chance to live, because you are alive."

She nodded into his shoulder. "I'm not going to keep doing this, keep feeling sorry for myself."

"No, you're not. Instead you're going to be the friend Amy expected you to be. You're going to face life and you're going to do it every single day, thinking that you have this chance, this moment, to be happy. Do it for her."

And then he kissed her, just a brief brush of his lips against hers.

"Thank you." She smiled as she said it. "I needed that."

He picked Cash up, settling him on his left hip and then reached for her hand with his right one. Together they crossed to the sidewalk where Callie was telling Bill about her kitten.

Normal returned with a rush and it felt good. It felt good even ten minutes later as they sat in the activity room where Doris was picking out a hymn on the old piano. Her left hand didn't quite keep up with the right but the melody carried down the hall, drawing a crowd.

Bill sang along, an old hymn about redemption. Dylan moved from Harmony's side and returned a minute later with a guitar that he held out to her. She looked up, unsure.

He winked and placed the guitar in her hands.

"I'm not a Cross."

"You are a Cross, and you have an audience of people who need this."

She nodded and somehow managed to find the tune, strumming gently until she picked it up and found the rhythm of the hymn Doris played. Bill smiled at her from the bench next to his wife. Harmony sang along, joining him on the chorus. And then she heard Dylan next to her, his voice a perfect tenor.

When the song ended, the crowd that had gathered clapped. Someone called out a request. Doris flipped through the song book and found "In The Sweet By and By," the requested song. As Harmony played, a few stray tears slipped down her cheeks. *We shall meet on that beautiful shore.* She thought of Amy there, and knew her friend wouldn't want to come back to this life, the heartache, the pain.

But she wanted Amy back.

Grief choked her but she managed to smile at the concerned look Dylan gave her. She nodded, letting him know she was okay. She felt pieces of herself coming back together, even with the pain, even with the tears. And wasn't that why she had come to Dawson in the first place, to find the person she used to be?

The one thing she hadn't expected was this friendship with Dylan Cooper and how it made her feel stronger.

* * *

"Will you come back next week?" One of the older men asked Dylan as he put up the guitar and picked up the pieces of a puzzle Cash had been playing with.

"'I think we might manage that." Dylan took the hand that was offered, shaking it.

"That would be real good." The gentleman moved his wheelchair closer. "And that's a pretty little wife and some sweet kids you've got."

Dylan choked a little. "She's not my wife. Just a friend."

"Well, if I was you, I wouldn't let her get away."

Dylan smiled because it seemed a lot easier than explaining. He turned and saw that Harmony had joined Cash and Callie at a table. They were stacking dominoes. She smiled up at him and then went back to playing with the kids. Bill had taken Doris back to her room.

As everyone left the room, Dylan sat in the empty seat next to Harmony. "They'd like for us to come back."

She didn't look up. "I know."

"I'm game if you are," he offered.

She laughed at something Cash did with the dominoes and then she looked up, her dark blue eyes smoky with emotion. "It's heartbreaking, isn't it?"

"Yeah, it is."

He didn't need for her to explain what she meant by that. Being here, seeing people who were lonely and alone, people forgetting who they used to be.

"I'd like to do this, Dylan. For as long as I'm here. These people need us." She stacked another domino. "I might need them, too."

His mind took an unexpected turn because lately,

when she mentioned leaving, he realized he wasn't looking forward to the day she packed up and went back to her life in Nashville. He didn't want to think about her being gone.

To make it easier he tried to tell himself it was for the kids, for Cash and Callie. She'd become pretty important to them. But Dylan had never been one to lie, not even to himself. She was becoming pretty important to him.

They waited at the front of the nursing home for Bill. He eventually joined them, looking a little worse for wear, Dylan thought. It couldn't be easy, leaving Doris here. It couldn't be easy, going home to that empty farmhouse.

"Let me give you a lift home, Bill," Dylan offered as he pushed the door open.

"That would be good of you, Dylan." Bill gave Harmony a cautious look. "Will that be okay with you, Miss Cross?"

"Of course it is, Bill. And please call me Harmony."

"I sure appreciate you stopping by today." He patted her arm, an awkward gesture, Dylan thought. He walked behind the two of them. Cash and Callie were holding his hands, and Cash was doing his favorite number, leaning to one side and pretending to go limp.

"Stand up and walk, Cash," Dylan warned with a smile. "Or I'll just have to throw you over my shoulder like a bag of flour."

"Flowder. Flowder." Cash giggled and let his knees buckle. Dylan lifted the little boy and tossed him over his shoulder, holding him by the ankles. Cash continued to laugh and then Callie mimicked her brother, letting her legs buckle.

"Another sack of flour?" Dylan grabbed up the little girl and let her hang over his other shoulder. "I'm not sure what I'll do with all this flour."

Harmony was telling Bill goodbye, her eyes bright and all of the shadows gone. He let the kids slide to the ground.

"I'll see you at church tomorrow?" Dylan asked as he opened the truck door. Cash clambered into his seat and Callie pulled the straps over his shoulder to buckle him in. As Dylan walked away he heard Cash telling his sister, "Me. Me."

Because all of a sudden the little guy wanted to do it on his own. Dylan followed Harmony to her car, remembering that he'd promised his mom something.

"Will you eat lunch with us at the ranch tomorrow?"

She had already opened her car door and she turned toward him. He had noticed earlier that her dark blue sundress made her eyes look like an evening sky. He noticed that she hadn't used her cane and that she now rested her left foot, putting most of her weight on her right leg.

He noticed a lot about Harmony Cross. He noticed that her lips parted, ever so slightly and a man could drown in the depths of those blue eyes. He also noticed that he'd been reduced to thinking poetic thoughts that would have his brothers giving him a hard time if they knew.

"I'm not sure."

"Big plans?"

"No, it just…" She looked away. "It's me. It just isn't that easy."

"I understand."

She looked up at him. "Thank you."

"You don't have to thank me. But if you are at church, the invitation to lunch still stands. And give yourself a break, Harmony. You should see yourself through my eyes, or through Cash and Callie's eyes. Even the eyes of the people in the nursing home. You're judging yourself pretty harshly, but you're not giving yourself much room for forgiveness."

"Maybe I don't deserve it."

"Oh, come on. You're punishing yourself for something you can't undo."

"But if I could…"

"You can't. What you *can* do is see that maybe you can be the person you were always meant to be. And that person has a gift that she's using to minister to people in this place. You're more than the mistakes you've made."

"That person is lucky to have you for a friend." She laced her fingers through his. "I should go. But thank you."

He should have walked away, but didn't. Instead he moved to brush his lips against her cheek. Somehow his mouth captured hers in the sweetest kiss. Her hand was still in his and he pulled her close. He moved his other hand to her back and felt her shiver beneath his touch.

Her lips parted beneath his and he drew in a breath, needing air, needing her. Every other sweet moment they had shared paled in comparison to this. Because this was real, more real than anything he'd ever experienced with any other woman. He slid his hand up her back, settling it between her shoulders. Her hair curled over his skin.

They were in a parking lot in front of the nursing home in the afternoon. As he kissed her, wanting to hold her close for a long time, he remembered. They also had truckloads of reasons for not getting involved.

For a few minutes it didn't matter. And for a few minutes he'd allowed himself to be a single man attracted to a beautiful woman. It had been a long time. Maybe that explained the need to hold her close, his lips now resting in her hair, close to her ear. He breathed in the soft scent of lavender.

Yes, that was it. He hadn't dated in over a year. Hadn't even thought about dating. Knowing that, he should be able to put things in perspective.

"Dylan." Her voice was shaky. "I should go."

He nodded, still holding her close. "Yes, you should."

He let her go, releasing her hand from his. She stepped back, composed, her breathing steady. He wanted her to be as unsettled as he was. Maybe she was. Maybe the way she avoided his gaze was Harmony unsettled, undone. He watched as she fidgeted and he tried to come up with the right words to say goodbye, or that he was sorry.

"Harmony…"

"Don't say something stupid."

He laughed a little. "Well, I'm not sure if I can say something intelligent."

"Then tell me you'll see me tomorrow and I'll get in my car and leave."

"I'll see you tomorrow."

She nodded at that. And then she didn't get in her car. She looked up at him, unsmiling. "And we won't do that again."

Dylan brushed a hand across his cheek and grinned. "I never make a promise I can't keep."

With that he walked away, chuckling a little because

he heard her exasperated sigh as she got in her car. Good, he was getting under her skin. That seemed only fair, because she was definitely getting under his.

And one promise he knew he could keep was that he would kiss her again. Soon.

Chapter Eleven

On her way to church the next morning, Harmony made a stop at the nursing home. She parked close to the door in the patient loading zone. She'd noticed Bill Tanner's truck parked a short distance away. She found the Tanners in the dining room. Breakfast was over and the tables were being cleared and reset for lunch. Doris smiled and waved when she saw Harmony.

"What are you doing here this morning?" Doris asked, her speech still halting from the stroke.

"I came to see if you'd like to go to church. I know Bill can sign you out of here, but I didn't know if you could get in his truck." Harmony smiled at Bill and he winked, actually winked. The gesture made it even easier for her to smile.

Being part of their lives made her feel as if she was a part of something real. She had the Tanners, she had Dylan and the kids. It was a life. Not the life she was used to, but maybe one that would begin her second chance. And it felt good.

"I think that would be dandy," Bill agreed with a

big smile. He reached to pat his wife's hand. "What do you think, Doris?"

"It would be good to go to church. They have services here, but isn't the same as being in my church." Doris smiled up at her husband, and Harmony felt a pang of envy.

She didn't allow the feeling to take root. Instead she helped Doris get ready, and then they loaded up in Harmony's car. Doris exclaimed over the interior. Bill grumbled as he climbed in the backseat.

A few minutes later they pulled in to a handicapped parking space at the church. A few people gave them looks. Harmony was used to the looks. She'd dealt with them since the accident. From the outside she looked healthy. She had a great car. She had a young body.

She shouldn't be parking in the handicapped space.

But as she put up the blue card, hanging it from her mirror, people always looked, they always talked. Sometimes she parked in regular parking, just to avoid the embarrassment.

Today she had Doris, though. She got out of the car and Bill was already getting Doris the wheelchair that they'd stowed in the trunk. He opened it and then helped his wife out, settling her in the seat, arranging her hair and her clothes.

"Look who made it to church!" The voice behind her nearly made Harmony jump, even though she recognized it almost immediately. She waved at Cash and Callie, then met Dylan's steady gaze.

"Look who nearly made me have a heart attack." She smiled as she said it.

"You picked up Doris!"

"You don't have to act so surprised." She stepped

onto the sidewalk, moving to catch up with Doris and Bill. But they were quickly surrounded by friends.

Dylan reached for her arm. "Do you want to go to the drive-in movie this evening?"

She glanced up, unsure. "There isn't a drive-in for miles around."

Callie started to say something but he stopped her with a finger to his lips. "Yes, there is," he said with a mysterious smile.

"Really? And what's showing?"

"I'm not really sure, but I can guarantee it'll probably be a cartoon."

She was curious, how could she not be. And curiosity had so often been her downfall. She sighed and gave in. "Okay, I'll go to the drive-in."

As they made their way up the ramp to the front doors of the church, Callie hung back, taking hold of her hand. Cash followed Dylan, helping him and Bill push Doris up the ramp. It felt like any other Sunday morning, really. It felt normal. It felt as if she had always been here, had always been this person who went to church, helped others, held the hand of a little girl.

She hadn't been this person in such a long time. She wanted to keep being this Harmony, not the one she'd left behind. As they walked through the front doors of the church, they were greeted by Pastor Wyatt Johnson.

Harmony remembered him as the young man who had team roped and chased girls. He'd been older than her, but she'd known him, and known the older girls who had chased him back.

"Harmony, good to see you here today." He shook Dylan's hand and then reached for hers. "Would Tuesday evening work for you?"

Had she signed up for something?

"The recovery program," Wyatt explained.

"Oh, of course. Tuesday." She remembered a conversation at the Mad Cow when they had discussed the program and she'd agreed to take part.

"Good. I'll have Rachel give you a call when we know for sure."

Before she could really think about what she had agreed to, a hand touched her arm, pulling her from thoughts that included how to get out of a local meeting. Harmony glanced up, expecting Dylan. Instead Myrna Cooper beamed at her. Her gray hair was short, her makeup perfect and a string of pearls hung from her neck.

"Mrs. Cooper, it's good to see you. I heard you were on a cruise." Harmony looked around, searching for Dylan, Cash or Callie. She'd been left alone, left in the clutches of a notorious matchmaker. Dylan should have known better.

"Why, Harmony Cross, you look wonderful. And yes, I have been on a cruise. Winston and I were married last spring and we've been having a wonderful time."

"I'm so happy for you."

Myrna slipped an arm through Harmony's, latching them together in a way that was unmistakable. "I'm happy for you, too. I hear you've been spending time with that grandson of mine. It's good that he has you to help him out."

"We've been helping each other out, Mrs. Cooper."

Myrna tsk-tsked a few times. "Harmony, you've known me too long to call me Mrs. Cooper. You can call me Granny Myrna. Besides, I'm not Mrs. Cooper.

I'm a married woman now. And let me tell you, there is nothing better than marriage to a good man." Myrna stopped and gave her a long look. "Now what is that frown for?"

"I didn't frown." Harmony managed a smile to prove her point.

"Why, honey, that's the most hangdog look on a young woman. As pretty as you are, there should be men waiting in line for you."

"I'm really not looking, Myrna."

"No, of course you aren't. But when you aren't looking, that's when the perfect man comes along and steals your heart."

Harmony looked around, wishing for an escape, not a man. Well, maybe a man to rescue her would be nice. Myrna pointed her toward empty seats near the rest of the Coopers. Dylan reappeared, this time without children.

She shot him a pleading look and he returned it with a grin that might have meant he was leaving her with his grandmother. At the last possible moment he moved to her side, claiming her.

They took their seats just as the choir stepped forward. Harmony looked around and saw that Bill and Doris had taken seats with friends. That left her to settle in next to Dylan, with Jackson Cooper on her other side.

Once upon a time she'd attended this church, sitting in a pew with her family. She'd never doubted God. Never doubted her faith. If someone had told her that there would be a day when she yelled at God, angry with her life, she never would have believed it.

It had all happened, but as she sat there listening to the sermon she realized that faith was coming back to her, slowly, piece by piece. She was trusting again. Maybe it was true, that when she made it through, she would be stronger. Her faith would be stronger.

A verse came to mind. *When you go through the fire, I will be with you.*

Dylan reached for her hand. She glanced at him, surprised by the gesture, more surprised by the look in his eyes. He wouldn't let her down, his expression said. But she could let him down. Didn't he see that?

His hand held hers tight, refusing to let her go. She squeezed his back, but avoiding looking at him again. Her heart ached, wishing she didn't have to let go. Ever.

After church Dylan had walked with Harmony to her car. He'd helped get Doris settled in the front passenger seat. He'd helped get her wheelchair in the trunk. He refrained from kissing Harmony goodbye as Bill had climbed in the back and she'd taken her seat behind the wheel.

He'd kept a good handle on his emotions, pretending he walked a woman to her car every Sunday and wished he didn't have to say goodbye. It had crept up on him, this need to hold her close. During the service he'd done a lot of praying for some common sense to get hold of his emotions. He knew he was impulsive. Impulsive had kept him in Texas for a little better than a year. Impulsive had been with him when he signed his name to legal papers giving him permanent custody of Callie and Cash.

Impulsive had taken hold of him when he proposed to Harmony. It had been a joke. He'd said it the way a person said something funny and impossible.

As much as he wanted to count Harmony off as another impulsive move in his life, she wasn't. He knew people would think she was. That's what they were used to from him. Some called him spontaneous. Others called him thoughtless or rash. Maybe he had doubts of his own. Of course he did. How could he trust his judgment when he'd spent almost twenty-eight years rushing into things because it felt right?

What he was coming to terms with was the fact that Harmony Cross felt more than right. She felt like forever. And it scared the daylights out of him.

He didn't want to rush things. And he didn't think she was ready to believe anyone wanted her in their lives forever. He had a strong suspicion that Harmony Cross doubted herself more than she let on.

What did surprise him was that she didn't show up for the movie at Cooper Creek. She had skipped out on lunch, telling him she planned on having lunch at the nursing home with Doris and Bill. But she had accepted the offer to eat dinner with his family and then watch a movie.

Callie had been allowed to pick out the movie while in town with Dylan's mom. The big screen was set up on the lawn, and there were lawn chairs and blankets to sit on. They'd made popcorn and thrown soda in the cooler. It mattered to him that Harmony show up.

When everyone started to ask questions, he made excuses. Said maybe she'd be a little late. He tried her cell phone and she didn't answer.

His family didn't say anything even though the sun had gone down and they were waiting. Dylan didn't want to admit, to them or to himself, but fear was knocking on the door with a pretty heavy hand.

There were a lot of what-ifs going through his mind

when his mom put a hand on his shoulder. "Go check on her. I'll watch Cash and Callie."

He did his best to pretend he wasn't waiting for her car to come up the drive. "I'm sure she's fine."

"Of course she is, but you're standing there worrying about everything that could be wrong, and if you don't go over there, you'll form conclusions."

"She's a grown woman."

"Yes, she is. Even grown women need help from time to time."

He grabbed his hat off the hook next to the door. I'll be back in a few minutes."

"We'll be here."

He jumped in his truck and headed toward the Cross Ranch. There were no lights on inside. The barn looked pretty quiet, too. Her car was in the driveway. He headed for the house. That's when he saw her on the porch. She smiled at him, wan, tired, close to tears.

"What are you doing here?" She evaded his gaze, and he wondered, was she good at hiding when she'd been using?

He sat down in the rocking chair next to hers, unsure. "I came for you. Do I need to call someone?"

She laughed a little but without humor. "Oh, welcome to 'this is your life with an addict, Dylan Cooper.' Always wondering, always doubting, always convinced they'll fall. For the first couple of months out of rehab, my parents monitored my phone calls, my texts and they regularly checked my room, my purse and my bathroom."

She paused, then said, "Not that I blamed them. It's what they had to do, even when it hurt."

He felt a sudden rush of anger that he hadn't expected

to feel. He had two kids waiting for a movie, waiting for her. He didn't have time for games.

"Funny, but I thought you were a recovering addict, not an addict."

"I'm 155 days clean. I mark the days off on a calendar. I'm fighting, Dylan. I came to Dawson because I wanted to fight in private."

"Did you…" he started to ask, but then didn't know if he wanted the answer.

She shook her head. "No, I didn't. I told you, I'm fighting."

"Why are you sitting out here?"

"Because when the pain is at its worst, I need a way to distract myself. I'm counting stars. I'm listening to crickets. I'm trying to get inside. This is as far as I could make it. And it seemed better out here, less lonely. The problem is, my phone is in there."

"What can I do?" His anger had already fled and in its place, concern.

She shook her head and he saw her stiffen, then pull her legs in close. She looked up at the darkening sky. "Promise me you won't stop being my friend. I've lost a lot of friends."

"I am your friend."

"I know that, but you have no idea how hard it is to stay in my life. I had a voice mail today from Amy's fiancé. He wanted me to know that if I hadn't called her for a ride, they would have been married."

He didn't have words to help her, not this time. He reached for her hand. "Let's go."

"Go? Haven't you heard me? I'm trying to tell you this is wrong. It isn't good for you. Tonight you wondered if I was using. You should be with Callie and Cash, not here worrying about me."

"I can do both."

"Where are they?"

She meant Callie and Cash. "With my mom, waiting."

"So now your family is pulled into the drama." She shook her head. "Don't you see? This isn't what I wanted for you, for your family. My life is all about drama. Amy told me that, you know. When she picked me up at the party, she told me I had to stop the drama and get help. She told me she couldn't help me anymore. It was the last time, she said. No more bailing me out, picking me up or rescuing me. No more being my enabler."

"I think you've got a few things wrong."

She looked up, barely smiling but it was enough. "What do I have wrong?"

"I'm not here to rescue you. I'm here because you told Cash and Callie you would watch a movie with them tonight. This isn't about you, it's about them. They need you in their lives."

She covered her face with her hands. "I forgot. I'm sorry, I messed up."

"Yeah, you messed up. So come on, let's go." He shoved aside sympathy because she didn't need it, she needed to live.

"You seem to think that's an option. But the problem is, I can't get up. I can't put weight on my left leg. That's why I'm out here."

"What happened?"

"I was in a car wreck." She smiled as she said it,

and he felt a rush of relief to see she still had a sense of humor.

"Good to know. I'm glad we're getting all of our baggage out in the open."

"Really, what's yours?"

"I'm in…" He'd almost said it. But he couldn't. Not right now. "I'm in need of some drama. So tell me what happened. Today, not the accident."

"I managed to get the lead rope on Beau, then he managed to yank me off my feet."

"Do we need to go to the ER, or call Jesse?" His brother the doctor was used to late-night calls from his accident-prone family.

"No need for either. I thought if I rested here a while, I'd be able to make it inside."

"How'd you get here from the barn?"

"It took me a while. By the time I got to the porch, I'd had enough."

He was out of the chair and he reached for her hand. "Let's see if you can stand up."

She took his hand. He helped her to her feet, then pulled her close and lifted her into his arms, cradling her against him. Her arms went around his neck. She was light in his arms and her hair brushed his face as she leaned into his shoulder. She smelled like lavender. Everything about her made him want to hold her close and never let go.

If he told her that, she'd demand he put her down.

"Where are we going?" she asked.

"To Cooper Creek for a movie. I'll make you chamomile tea and we'll have popcorn with chocolate. What you need is a cartoon about miniature plant people living in a forest."

"I love miniature plant people."

He pulled the driver's-side truck door open and deposited her in the seat as gently as he could. "I bet you do."

He slid in next to her and she didn't bother moving to the far side of the truck. Instead she stayed tucked close to his side. He shifted and then wrapped an arm around her shoulder, pulling her against him.

He could get used to this woman riding next to him. He could get used to her needing him.

"Does this happen often?" He asked as they headed the short distance down the road to his place.

She shrugged the shoulder that nestled against his side. "It isn't as bad as it was. The first couple of months after the accident I was in a wheelchair. There were months on crutches. Now I'm down to the cane most of the time. They say I'll keep getting stronger and the pain will lessen. I'm never going to be the person I was a year ago. Maybe that's a good thing."

He listened, knowing this was another of her warnings to him. Don't get too attached, she was telling him. He should heed the warnings.

When they got to Cooper Creek, he lifted her out of the truck and carried her to a waiting lawn chair. She looked up at him, her eyes bright, her face flushed pale in the moonlit night. He considered leaning to kiss her. He almost whispered that she couldn't scare him off.

Cash tackled him out of nowhere. Toddler arms wrapped around his legs, just in the nick of time. He smiled down at the little boy who had just kept him from saying things that he definitely shouldn't be saying, not yet.

Maybe not ever.

Chapter Twelve

The night air was cool, seeping into Harmony's bones. But there were outdoor heaters and blankets, and she had Callie in her lap. The cartoon was funny and sweet, even bringing tears to her eyes in places. Next to her, Dylan whispered a teasing comment from time to time, but usually got silenced by his mother or one of his sisters. There were probably two dozen people watching the movie.

When the credits rolled, Callie slid off her lap, still clutching the blanket they'd been using. Cool air hit and Harmony shivered. Dylan stood, holding Cash, who had fallen asleep in his arms. She smiled up at the cowboy and the little boy he held against his shoulder. He was good and kind.

Callie climbed her way into his free arm and he held them both, shaking his head as he looked down at her. She knew what he was thinking, that she would need help, too.

"I've got this," she spoke softly, wanting to keep it between the two of them.

Around them the Coopers were scattering, grabbing

chairs, blankets and the younger children who hadn't made it through the entire movie. A few shot curious glances in Harmony's direction. They probably wondered about her, what she was doing here. What was she doing with Dylan?

They probably thought she would hurt him. She worried about the same thing. She could see the change in their relationship. She saw that look in his eyes, the one that said he would protect her, take care of her.

Fix her.

She didn't want that from him. And she'd seen in his eyes tonight when he'd first showed up to get her that he also knew she could let him down.

It was a hard lesson to learn but better that he learned it now. She pushed herself up and stood gingerly, knowing there would be pain, knowing her muscles would protest. It hurt, but it wasn't the worst pain.

"I should have brought my car."

He shook his head, "I'll give you a ride home. Let me get these two in the truck."

She nodded and he walked away. And then Angie Cooper was at her side. With her soft smile and knowing look.

"Thank you for including me." Harmony held the back of the chair and smiled at her hostess. "I'm sorry for keeping everyone later than they expected."

"Don't apologize. We're a big family and nothing ever runs on schedule." Angie slipped an arm around her waist. "Why don't you stay here tonight?"

She looked up at the big brick home with its welcoming front porch and white columns. "Angie, I'm fine."

"I know you are, but I also know you aren't feeling the best. Why not stay here where there are other people?"

The offer hung between them, and then Dylan was there. He must have overheard because he smiled and took her hand in his.

"It's pointless to argue." He leaned close to her ear and whispered. His breath was warm, and she shivered.

"Is it?" Harmony slipped her fingers through his. "I really am okay."

"Stay here." He held her hand close to his side. "Mom can make you some chamomile tea. It will help you sleep. If you wake up tomorrow and need anything, she'll be here."

Oh, the things she needed. She smiled up at the man who thought he knew, but he didn't. She hadn't come here expecting him. She'd come expecting a few weeks of solitude, thinking privacy was what she needed. She hadn't expected to find friends. She hadn't expected her faith to return the way it had. She hadn't expected any of this. She hadn't known she needed this place so much.

"I'll go inside and get a downstairs room ready for you, Harmony." Angie Cooper didn't take no for an answer. "Dylan can help you inside."

"The kids are in the truck waiting," Harmony reminded him as they started toward the house. He led her to the backyard, and the back door.

"I'm taking Heather home. She's in the truck with them. Her car wouldn't start. Alternator, I think."

"I see."

The back door led them through a utility room. Dylan reached to flip on a light, but his hand froze, and he looked at her. Pale moonlight slipped through the curtains, bathing the room in a silver glow, and still he didn't flip the switch. Instead his hand moved from the wall to her cheek. He settled his lips against hers. She kissed him back, hungry for the warmth that came from being held in his arms. His hands brushed through her hair, his fingers threading through the curls. She shivered beneath his touch.

"Dylan." She shook her head, pulling away from him. "No."

"Yes," he mumbled as he kissed her again. "Yes."

"Your mom…"

"Is understandably avoiding the utility room because I'm a grown man and you're a grown woman. We aren't kids sneaking around, hiding behind trees."

"No, that was ten years ago."

He chuckled a little. "Yeah and if I'd had any sense, I wouldn't have told you I didn't mean it."

"Did you?"

He kissed her again and then he smiled, still with his lips against hers. "Yes."

She backed away, stumbling a little. He caught her close.

"This is too much, Dylan. I can't do this. Not yet." And who was she to have this moment, this man, when she had a message on her answering machine from another man, one who wouldn't have moments with the woman he loved.

The cold reminder did what nothing else could have. It pushed her from Dylan's arms. She didn't deserve his touch, his warmth.

"This is a relationship between friends, remember. We're helping each other out. We have to remember that." She eased away from him as she said it, holding the wall for support.

Angie appeared in the hall holding crutches and smiling. She looked at her son, a warning look, Harmony thought. And she wondered about that look. Was Angie Cooper warning her son to avoid danger, or warning him to give Harmony a break?

"We always have a pair of crutches around here, Harmony. And I think you might need them tonight?"

She took them, humiliated, sad, sorry to let go of something she knew could have been amazing. "Thank you."

"See you in the morning," Dylan called out as she headed toward the kitchen.

She glanced back over her shoulder. "In the morning?"

"We were going to plan Cash's birthday party. We need to run into Grove, pick a cake, the works."

Of course they were. And of course they had a deal and he wasn't letting her out of it. "Of course."

A few minutes later she heard the back door close, and Angie Cooper entered the kitchen. Harmony had taken a seat at the table on the other side of the room. Angie smiled when she saw her.

"I'm going to make you some tea. Maybe that will help you relax and sleep." As she said it, Angie rummaged in a cabinet, pulled out a box of tea and then filled a cup with water.

"Thank you." Harmony ran her hand over the smooth wood of the table. "Angie, Dylan and I are just friends. I want you to know that. I know everyone thinks, maybe we've let them think…"

Angie put the cup in the microwave and turned around.

"Harmony, you don't have to explain."

"I do. I know how it looks and I know you must be worried that Dylan…"

Angie shook her head. "No, I'm not worried. I'm not worried about Dylan. I'm not worried about you. Whatever arrangement the two of you have, I'm happy you have each other."

The microwave dinged and she pulled out the cup of tea.

"But we *don't* have each other."

Angie set the cup of tea down in front of her and she took the seat at the end of the table. "Oh, I think you do. I'm not new at this mom thing, Harmony. I've got a dozen kids and we've been through everything together. I have a daughter who recently told me she's tried to find a man and fall in love but she's decided being single is the best alternative for her. I have a son in South America because he feels responsible for the death of a friend. I have a son whose wife admitted to us just months ago that she is an alcoholic." Angie's brows inched up a notch and she smiled. "Surprised by how real the Coopers are?"

Harmony shook her head as she mulled the information and then she met the kindness in Angie's eyes. "No, I'm not surprised. I know that you are real and you're kind."

"And real means that we have real sins, real forgiveness and a very real attitude toward life. We all make mistakes. We all stumble and fall. We choose to stay down or get back up. You are on your feet, Harmony, and moving forward. It doesn't mean you won't fall from time to time, but it's all about being real with the people in your life, being able to tell the truth and ask for help when you need help."

Harmony sipped at the tea. And looked up, meeting Angie's steady gaze. "Thank you. I think that Dawson is helping me find the person I used to be. She kind of got lost in everything else I was going through."

"She was never lost." Angie patted her hand. "You were just determined to turn her into someone else. It happens to all of us. Pain can make us do crazy things. I almost left my husband once, years ago. And now, because I didn't, we have this life and we have children and grandchildren. We won because I didn't quit."

Pain makes a person do crazy things, Angie had said. As Harmony settled into bed a short time later she thought about the pain, and how it had started long before the accident. The emotional pain, not knowing how she fit in a family of people who seemed perfect. The pain of being abandoned, though, had been the pain that started it all. She was the Cross who shouldn't have been a Cross. She was the child rejected by a mother who couldn't love her enough to stay clean.

The emotional pain had been covered up with rebellion and alcohol. The physical pain, and the pain of losing Amy, had been covered up with pills.

She knew the steps to recovery. She knew how to move forward. She also knew that, no matter what Angie Cooper said, she couldn't put Dylan or his two precious kids in the path of destruction that was her life.

Dylan led Cash and Callie through his parents' house the next morning. He heard his mom singing to the radio, then listened as another voice joined hers. He smiled at the duet and peeked around the kitchen door to watch. Callie raced into the room, ending the song. Cash followed hot on her heels. Dylan knew a moment when everything felt right. His life. These two kids. It was starting to feel like well-worn boots, not someone else's shoes.

This morning he'd woken up a little late and Cash had somehow climbed out of his crib and run through the bedroom door to jump on him. Callie had stood at the door, unsure. She'd looked a little sad before jumping on the bed.

His kids.

His mom paused a moment while pouring pancake batter on the griddle. She nodded toward the coffeepot. "Help yourself."

"Thanks." He walked into the room trying to avoid Harmony with her hair long and curly around her face and a sundress that fit a little too loose, probably one left behind by one of his sisters. They were all a little taller than she was.

"Good morning," Harmony spoke softly. "Do you want the sugar?"

He shook his head as he poured coffee. "No, I take it just the way it is. Do you kids want juice or milk?"

"Juice," both said in loud unison, although Cash maybe said, "Joosh."

"Good, juice and maybe a quiet, inside voice." He shook his head, put his coffee cup down and opened the fridge. "Orange or grape?"

One of each. He turned toward the counter and Harmony had gotten two plastic cups out for him. He started to comment that she seemed very at home here. But he let it go.

He didn't know why he was so testy this morning. Maybe because he hadn't slept well. Maybe because he hadn't expected her in this kitchen with his mom, as if she belonged here in his life.

But hadn't he just been thinking last night that he wanted her in his life? He shook his head as he poured the juice and Harmony gave him a cautious look. He managed a smile for her because he definitely didn't want her to ask him what was wrong.

His life was just starting to feel like his life again, and here she was shaking it all up. He knew she had warned him. She'd been right. He didn't need his life, or Cash and Callie's lives, put back on the spin cycle. They'd been through enough. Like him, they were starting to adjust.

All of that made sense but then she walked by him, her arm brushing his. He wanted to pull her close, breathe her in, sweep her off her feet and head to Eureka Springs for a spur-of-the-moment wedding in some Victorian chapel.

"I've got to get out to the barn," he mumbled instead. "Mom, can you watch the kids for a few?"

"I can."

Harmony took the cups to the kids who were now sitting at the table.

"Thanks. I need to help Jackson and Gage move some round bales and then we're going to move some cattle to another field. It looks like it will be a pretty full morning."

"Did you still need my help?" She shot a look in Cash's direction. Not that a two-year-old cared if they talked about his party, but Dylan appreciated her effort to be discreet.

He shook his head. "I'll have to do it later."

"I can order the cake for you, if you'd like. Trains, right?"

"Trains. Are you sure you don't mind?"

"I really don't."

He watched as she carried plates of pancakes to Cash and Callie. He saw her limp, watched as she barely touched the counter for support. He felt like a creep. He opened his mouth to say something, to apologize for his bad mood.

"I should go," he said instead.

His mom handed him a breakfast sandwich on the way out the back door. "Eat something."

He took the offering and kissed her cheek. "Thanks, Mom."

"Be in a better mood when you come back in or you'll get nothing for lunch."

"You know I'm not a morning person."

She followed him to the back door where the two of them were alone. "No, you've always been a grouch in the morning. But that doesn't excuse your rude behavior this morning. Figure out what you're doing here, Dylan, before there's a whole mess of people hurt. Remember, it isn't just you now."

"I know that." Man, how he knew it.

As he headed for the barn the dog joined him. The border collie wagged his tail and barked a few times before running on ahead. It wasn't just him now.

The truth of his mom's warning hit him hard. This is what it meant when something came at a guy from left field. Unexpected.

Harmony was in the house, wondering what she'd done wrong and really, he couldn't think of anything. He had his own stuff to figure out, he guessed.

She had hers.

They had both hit some pretty serious walls in the last year. So maybe Harmony had been right, pulling back and not stepping too deep into his life. Maybe he'd been wrong, rushing forward toward something that felt right at the moment.

He headed for the barn and saw Gage walk out the side door, whistling a song and looking altogether too happy. Layla and Gage were expecting a baby. They were as happy as two people could be.

Dylan wanted that. He'd never realized that he wanted it. He wanted someone to come home to. He wanted someone to have babies with. Yeah, he wanted the whole package. Cash and Callie should have a real family, a mom and dad and siblings.

"Hey, you here to help?" Gage asked as he headed for the tractor parked next to the barn.

"Yeah, I guess I am. What do you want me to do?"

Gage turned to look at him. "You're such a morning person."

"No, I'm really not." Dylan picked up a stick and tossed it for the dog. "I'm here to work, if you let me know what to do."

"We're going to finish baling that hay on the forty acres behind the house. And then I guess we'll move the bales on the twenty."

"I'll start moving those bales if you're going to take the baler. Pretty decent hay for a fall crop." Dylan started toward the barn. "Where's Jackson?"

"Inside, figuring out what bulls we're taking to Oklahoma this weekend."

"Gotcha. Okay, I'll start moving bales."

"You okay?" Gage called out as he walked away.

Dylan shot his brother a look. "I said I'm fine."

Gage laughed at that. "Right, okay, we'll go with that answer. But if you need anything…"

It irked him that his little brother thought that because he was married he could give advice. He shook his head as he climbed inside the farm truck parked in front of the barn. He was just fine. Yeah, sure his insides were twisted in knots, but he could handle that. He could handle the thought of Harmony packing up and leaving in a few weeks and how much it was going to hurt Cash and Callie.

How much it was going to hurt him.

Chapter Thirteen

Doris put away the crochet she'd been trying to explain to Harmony. "You're not listening."

Harmony smiled. It was Tuesday and she was going to the recovery meeting in thirty minutes. She had to admit the idea was consuming her thoughts for the moment. And Doris should be the focus of her attention. Doris who had agreed to teach her to crochet.

"I'm sorry. I've always been knitting-and-crochet challenged."

"Because you have other things on your mind. The lovely thing about crocheting, Harmony, is that you can lose yourself for an hour or two. You can focus on the yarn and what you're creating. And not think."

To not think. Harmony loved the concept. She'd love to turn off her mind for a few hours and not think. Not think about the future, the past, the nightmares. The nightmares weren't as bad as they had been, though. Maybe time had helped. Or maybe she was finally coming to terms with the accident.

Doris patted her hand. "Stop thinking."

Harmony nodded and managed a smile. "So, they're

going to let you start going home on weekends. I bet Bill is happy."

"Happy and scared. But I'm doing so much better. I'm not in that chair anymore, just using this walker. I can talk again. I'm so ready to go home."

"I know you are." Because Harmony remembered first the physical-rehab facility after the accident and then drug rehab. She knew how it felt to be in a place like this, unable to really care for herself the way she once had, unable to walk out the door, unable to find a place to be alone.

And lonely. She knew how it felt to be lonely even when surrounded by people.

"There you go again. You are distracted today."

She managed another granny square because they'd decided she couldn't crochet a straight line. "I have a group meeting in thirty minutes."

"You'll be just fine, Harmony. You're strong."

"Thank you for thinking that."

"It's the truth. Sweetheart, you need to believe in yourself. But you also need to have faith."

"I'm getting there."

"It isn't always easy." Doris put her nearly finished afghan on the bed next to her. "I can admit I've been angry with God. I've been hurt. And I've found it is so much easier when I give myself over to His love. Let Him give you peace. Stop acting like you don't deserve it."

Did she deserve peace? She drew in a breath, fighting the sting of tears that came without warning.

"Doris, I think there was more to me pulling up your drive that day than to just buy a horse."

"Of course there was. And it isn't just about you,

Harmony. I can't imagine us going through this without you, and because of you we also have Dylan. It's…" Doris sniffled a little. "It's like having family. The two of you mean so much to us."

Harmony stood and leaned to kiss Doris's cheek. "You mean a lot to me, too."

"Go, you're going to make me cry." Doris shooed her away. "And when you go to this meeting, think about what I've said to you."

She nodded, hugged Doris one last time and left. As she walked down the hall and out the front door, she thought about how much stronger she was. She was stronger physically, emotionally and maybe spiritually. When she went home, back to Nashville, she would be able to start over with that in mind. She knew herself better than she had before the accident.

A few minutes later she pulled up to Back Street Community Center, where the recovery meetings had been moved to. There were a dozen cars in the parking lot. Harmony parked and as she did she saw Lucky Cooper's wife. The other woman smiled at her and waited on the sidewalk. Angie Cooper's daughter-in-law who was struggling with alcoholism. Now Harmony understood. Every family had struggles.

"I'm glad you could make it," Eva Cooper, Lucky's wife, said as she walked next to Harmony. "It gets easier."

"I hope so." Harmony drew in a breath and straightened her shoulders. She could do this.

And she did do it. She walked through the doors, smiled at the people sitting at tables, smiled at Wyatt Johnson and took a seat next to Eva.

The group started with music and prayer. Wyatt

Johnson explained that the group was about coming together to face emotional pain, addiction, and other behaviors that led to broken lives. Harmony thought maybe she fit in all categories. How to go forward with a broken life, a broken heart—that was the message of the day. It was a message for her life, she thought.

At the end of the meeting Eva Cooper sang a song that fit the theme, about knowing that in all things we know we can survive loss and that we can be held by God. Even when a person feels as if they have failed, they can still have God's love.

Somehow Harmony found herself at the altar, pouring her pain out to God, allowing Him to take it from her. She knew as Eva prayed with her that this was the first time she'd really allowed God to take the pain. She'd been holding on, punishing herself with it, knowing she deserved to feel pain.

As she stood Eva hugged her tight and told her this was a step forward. The others had left. The two of them walked out of the building, leaving Wyatt to lock up. Eva gave her a hug when they reached the parking lot.

"Call if you need anything," Eva offered.

"Thank you, I will."

"And when you do leave, make sure you find a good program in Nashville."

"I'll do that."

A truck pulled in the parking lot. Eva gave her a look. "I think someone is here to see you."

"Some people don't know what's good for them."

Eva laughed at that. "Are you talking about yourself or my brother-in-law?"

"Your brother-in-law, of course."

Eva left and Harmony walked to her car, unlocking the door and waiting. She didn't have to wait long. Dylan stepped out of his beat-up old truck and headed her way. His jeans were smudged with dirt and there was a rip in the elbow of his shirt. But he looked good, even with the five-o'clock shadow covering his cheeks.

"You look like you've been dragged through the dirt."

He brushed at the dirt on his jeans and smiled up at her. "We've got a couple of new bulls. It's been a long day."

"Are the kids with you?"

"Heather has them. I'm heading that way to get them. I thought maybe I'd pick up fried chicken at the Mad Cow and bring it over to your place for dinner."

"Dylan, I don't know."

"You have to eat. Callie misses you." He shrugged and grinned. "I miss you. And I thought we'd work with Beau."

He knew she wouldn't turn down the offer to work with her horse. "I can brush him now without any problems."

"He's coming along."

She didn't know what else to say. She'd just had a major revelation about herself, about punishing herself by holding on to the pain. Not that the grief would go away that easily, but she was coping. What did she do about Dylan?

"You're not going to turn down fried chicken, are you?"

She slid behind the wheel of her car and smiled up at him. "Sounds good. See you in thirty minutes?"

"That sounds about right."

And then he walked away, a cowboy who knew how

to be a dad, how to be a friend, and how to make her feel safe. She didn't think he'd planned it this way.

But it had happened. It was happening.

Dylan helped Callie and Cash out of his truck. He was really going to have to trade the two-door for a four-door. After the kids were on the ground and heading for Harmony's front door, he reached in and pulled out the to-go container that Vera had filled with fried chicken, mashed potatoes and gravy. The aroma had filled the cab of his truck and his stomach growled in response.

Harmony met him at the front door. She leaned against the door frame and he knew, because he'd been watching her, that she did this when she was worn-out from a long day. The kids were already inside, pulling toys and books out of a box she'd filled for them. A lamp glowed from the corner, casting the room in warm light. Harmony stepped away from the door and Dylan offered her a hand that she took without arguing.

"Thank you." She didn't look up as she said it.

The two of them made their way to the dining room off the big country kitchen. The table had been set.

It all looked a little too much like a home where a family belonged. As they sat down to eat, it started to rain. Harmony reached for his hand and then took Callie's hand on her left side.

He took the hint, removed his hat and bowed his head. A whole bunch of thoughts crowded a mind that should have been focused on thanking the Good Lord for his blessings. Two kids that smiled more. A woman sitting next to him, her hand in his.

Somehow he managed a prayer that thanked God but didn't get too specific.

Thunder crashed outside, rattling the windows. Lightning streaked across the sky. Callie looked up, a mouth full of chicken, her eyes widening at the continuing ruckus of the storm.

"It's just rain, Callie." He nodded at her plate. "Go ahead and eat."

"It's scary," she whispered, moving a little closer to Harmony's side.

"If you close your eyes and listen, it's a good sound." Harmony led by example, closing her eyes and looking peaceful. "Hear the rain on the roof?"

She looked down at Callie and smiled. Callie still had her eyes closed but she didn't look convinced of Dylan's way of thinking. Callie looked up, shaking her head.

"It's still scary."

"Keep your eyes closed and listen. Rain is like music. And the rain makes everything grow, even flowers."

Callie sighed and eventually the fear passed. He thought about Harmony, and how often she had to convince herself the fear or pain she felt wasn't real. The other night she'd told him counting stars gave her something to focus on. And now she was having Doris teach her to crochet. Another distraction.

Harmony finished eating and stood to carry her plate to the kitchen. She took Dylan's empty plate and the plastic plate Cash had used. Callie was still eating chicken.

"I'm going to help Harmony do the dishes, Callie. You finish eating, okay?"

"But the storm." Callie looked up at him, eyes wide with fear.

"The storm is outside and we're all right here together."

"Okay." But she didn't sound convinced.

Dylan walked into the kitchen where Harmony was loading the dishwasher. He saw what she needed, a kitchen stool in the corner of the room. He brought it to her and the cane that had been leaning against the pantry.

"Sit."

"You're bossy." But she didn't argue. She peered past him, smiling at something she saw in the dining room.

Dylan looked, to make sure everything was okay, that Cash hadn't climbed onto the ceiling fan or something equally dangerous. Callie had moved to Cash's side and was sitting close, telling him he didn't have to be afraid of the storm.

"Mommy's in heaven and storms come from heaven." Callie's voice was soft, her hand patting Cash's.

Dylan closed his eyes, wishing kids didn't have to suffer that kind of pain. Harmony leaned her head against his shoulder and her arm wrapped around him, pulling him close.

"They're getting through it the way kids do, by making sense of it."

He glanced down at her and he saw in her eyes the pain of understanding. Of course she knew what it was like to be a little girl left alone. But in a way that he couldn't even begin to imagine.

"Don't kiss me, Dylan."

He backed away, surprised by the order, surprised that it was exactly what he'd planned to do. He'd been close and she was easing herself off the stool and returning to the dishwasher.

"Don't kiss you?"

She loaded the few glasses in the sink and closed

the door of the dishwasher. "No more. We have to stop. Somewhere along the way, our perfect plan has turned into a perfect mess."

"It might be messy but I didn't think it was a mess."

She leaned on the cane and walked past him, to the fridge. She put away ketchup and juice before looking at him again.

"It is a mess and you know it. We're making it messy by letting ourselves think that what we started out with has become real. We've crossed the lines."

"I've always been bad at not staying in the lines," he teased.

She shot him a warning look. And then Callie was calling out to them, telling them Cash wanted out of the high chair and the lightning was really bad. So much for working with the horse.

Dylan helped Cash down from the high chair. When he turned back around Callie had hold of Harmony's hand, trying to convince her she was afraid of storms, too.

"I promise I'm not afraid of storms, Callie."

Dylan guessed she probably wasn't, but he knew something she was afraid of. She was afraid of what she was feeling. She was afraid of letting him—them— in her life.

"Can I stay the night with Harmony?" Callie asked, still holding on to Harmony's hand like it was a life preserver.

Dylan looked at Harmony, and she nodded. "I guess you can," he answered.

Callie looked up at Harmony, big eyes and serious intent. "I can sleep in her bed and she can tell me a story."

Dylan agreed. "Yes, she can."

Those were the things a little girl missed, he guessed. He tried but he knew he didn't always get it right. Katrina had taught him to do her hair. She'd taught him about dresses, little-girl shoes and the right soaps to use.

The rest had been up to him to learn. Katrina had left them way too soon. She should have had more years with her kids. She should have watched them grow up. It wasn't fair that she'd had to leave them with him.

He heard Harmony tell Callie she'd put on a movie for them, and yes, Callie could pick a cartoon. And then a hand touched his, leading him back to the dining room.

"Are you okay?" she asked, her hand still on his.

He looked down at the woman standing with bare feet, a long dress swishing around her legs. "What?"

"You left us for a minute in there."

He sighed. "Yeah, I guess I did. I was just thinking about all Katrina missed out on and everything the kids will miss with her not being here. Callie misses her the most."

"She was older. She remembers more about having a mommy."

Yeah, she had memories of Katrina, that was a good thing. She had memories, a bad thing. He had memories, too. One of Katrina making him promise to marry someone who would love her kids. Someone who would be a real mom to them, she'd said. Because she'd had a stepmother who hadn't loved her. Katrina had run away at fifteen and lived a rough life for a few years.

"I should go. Cash is getting sleepy."

Harmony touched his cheek and then she surprised him by standing on tiptoe and pulling him down to kiss him on the chin. He smiled at the sweet gesture.

"It will all work out." Harmony walked with him back to the living room. Callie was curled up on the sofa and Cash was pushing a toy car across the floor making the appropriate sounds. Callie told him to drive a more quiet car and Cash giggled.

Yeah, he guessed it would all work out. But for now he had to pick Cash up and walk out into the rain. As they went out the door, he dropped his hat on Cash's head to protect him from the downpour. Dylan glanced back to see Callie wrap her arms around Harmony's waist. Harmony hugged her back.

It would all work out.

Chapter Fourteen

It was October, and Harmony's time in Dawson would come to an end soon. She sat next to Doris, crocheting colorful granny squares and thinking about what it would be like to go home, to Tennessee. When she thought of home, though, she thought Dawson. She didn't think about the large home her parents lived in, or her own apartment in Nashville.

Home had become the farmhouse her dad was considering putting on the market. Home was Dawson Community Church and the Mad Cow Café. Doris, Heather, Eva, these were her friends, the people who didn't expect more than she could give. They gave what she needed and were honest with their opinions.

She'd spent the better part of her life never knowing who liked her for herself and who wanted to be close to her because it might help them. Other than her family, Amy and these people in Dawson, she hadn't had a lot of honest relationships.

The buzz of her cell phone cut into the peaceful silence. She reached into her purse and saw her mother's name and picture flash across the screen. She answered with a smile.

"Hi, Mom."

"Hey, honey. How are you?"

"Good. I'm learning to crochet. You'll be proud. I'm making you an olive-green afghan for Christmas. With peach trim. Promise me you'll put it on your bed."

Olivia Cross laughed. "It isn't really olive-green, is it?"

"No, you'll like it. What's up?"

And then Olivia Cross gave her an address in Missouri, a place less than two hours away from Grove and Dawson. It was where Patricia Duncan now lived. Olivia said something about homeless shelters in Texas and Kansas, then moving to Springfield and finally to a small town outside of Joplin. She worked at a hotel, in housekeeping. Harmony listened, her heart beating rapidly as the news sank in.

"How did you find her?"

"Lila helped me. It took a while but we found her. I'm going to call her. But I wanted to let you do this first. I want this to be between the two of you."

"Okay." Harmony drew in a breath. "Mom, thank you. I love you."

"I love you, too. Call me after you see her, because I know you're going now."

"I am."

There was a long pause and then her mother sighed softly into the phone. "Do you want to wait and I'll go with you?"

"No, I think I need to face her alone."

"I understand. But Harmony, I need for you to re-member something. Remember that you're our daughter in every way that matters. From the moment you walked into our lives, you have been ours."

"I know."

She ended the call and dropped her phone back in her purse. Doris was watching her, questioning looks in her deep gray eyes.

"My birth mother lives less than two hours from here. All of this time and she's right here."

"Goodness."

"I should be excited to see her, right?"

Doris stopped crocheting. "I think you'd feel a lot of things right now, Harmony. I'm not sure if excited would be the word."

"I'm afraid that if I look at her, I'm going to see myself."

"Oh, hogwash." Doris dropped her yarn and crochet hooks in the basket next to her chair. "You're not her. I'm not sure why you have such a poor opinion of yourself."

"I think it comes from being raised surrounded by spectacular people. My sister is unbelievably beautiful and intelligent, Doris. My brother has our dad's talent. I'm the middle child in all ways. I'm medium."

Doris shook her head, then laughed a little. "I think you are spectacular, Harmony. How many young women your age are spending their days at a nursing home doing senior Zumba, or taking meals to a cranky old farmer? You're as spectacular as they come. And you need to spend a little time believing in yourself. Don't you dare decide your future based on what has happened in the past or on the woman who gave birth to you."

"Doris, I wish I could take you with me everywhere I go."

"You'll always have me, honey. You just have to stop by and visit or give me a call. I'll tell you how the cow ate the cabbage. And I promise you, if I think you're messing up, I'll tell you that, too."

"I'm counting on it." She looked at her watch and stood to go. "I guess I'm going to make a trip to Missouri."

"Why don't you take someone with you?"

"No, I think I have to do this alone."

Doris shook her head. "I know I can't convince you otherwise."

Harmony leaned to kiss her friend's cheek. "Not this time."

She left, walking out into bright fall sunshine, the sky a brilliant blue. The summer haze had long gone, and the air felt free from humidity with a hint of a north wind that made long sleeves feel good.

As she crossed the parking lot to her car, she noticed the new dark blue Ford pulling in but didn't think much about it. Not until it parked next to her and she looked up did she realize that the cowboy behind those tinted windows was the last cowboy she wanted to see. He smiled at her as he got out. She opened her door and pretended the week since the storm had been a good week. A week in which the two of them had been moving toward independence. Because she'd pointed out to him the day after Callie's sleepover that they needed to prepare the kids for when she left town.

The deciding factor had been when Callie cuddled up with her that night and said she wanted her to be her new mommy.

"How's Doris?" Dylan asked as he approached her.

"Good. Nice truck."

"Thanks. I finally retired my old truck. I bought that thing with cattle money when I was sixteen and it lived a long and useful life."

"Not an easy life, I'm sure."

He grinned at that. "No, not always an easy life. Where you heading to?"

She almost told him. Almost. "Home. Where are Cash and Callie?"

He rounded the front of her car and she wished she'd already gotten behind the wheel. Instead she found herself trapped by a man who was so casual about his good looks and charm that she found it hard to take a deep breath when he was around.

"They're with my mom. I've been out at Camp Hope helping Gage put together some team-building exercises for troubled teens that'll be there at the end of the month for a weekend retreat."

Camp Hope was a local camp started by football player Adam MacKenzie. He'd grown up in the area and moved back after retiring from a pro football career. He'd married a local, Jenna Cameron.

"I heard a rumor that you're leaving at the end of the month." He switched the conversation back to a subject she'd hoped they could avoid.

"I am." She bit down on her bottom lip and looked off in the direction of the field behind the nursing home. "Dylan, please don't."

"I'm not doing anything, Harmony. I was just going to say that we're friends, and you should treat me like a friend."

"I know. It isn't easy saying goodbye. It isn't easy

knowing that I won't be here and Callie might want her hair done and Cash might eventually say my name."

"It isn't supposed to be easy to walk away from people you care about."

Ouch. That hurt and from the look he gave her, he knew it.

"I'm not walking away, I'm going home."

"Yeah, I guess you are. For some reason, I thought this was home."

"It's *your* home."

He shook his head, adjusted his white cowboy hat and then pinned her with a glare. "You're one stubborn female, you know that?"

"I know. But I'm also the woman trying hard not to let you down." She tried to change the subject. "By the way, I ordered the cake, like you asked. And I'll be here for Cash's birthday. If I'm still invited."

"You know you are."

He leaned in, resting one arm across the top of her car. "I wish you'd give yourself a chance. I wish…"

"What?"

He shook his head. "Nothing. I need to go see Doris. I built a ramp for her, just in case she needs it when she goes home. Bill is out buying groceries, hoping that by next week she'll be home for good."

"I hope she is. I know they miss each other."

"Yeah, that's how it is when you care about someone."

"See you later, Dylan."

"See you later, Princess." He closed her door and stepped back as she drove away.

She hadn't left Dawson yet and she already missed him. She hadn't expected to feel this way, but she did.

And she couldn't tell him where she was going, because he had his own life to deal with. She couldn't be one more person Dylan Cooper felt he had to take care of.

Dylan rapped on the door of Doris's room and when she answered, he took his hat off and walked in. Her roommate, an older woman who never left the bed, glared at him. He smiled and nodded at her. But she couldn't be charmed.

"Dylan, it's so good to see you. You just missed Harmony."

"I saw her in the parking lot. How are you doing, Doris? Ready to go home soon?"

"I'm very ready to go home. I'm going to miss Harmony, though." She smiled at him. "I bet you and the kids will miss her, too."

He raked his fingers through his hair and leaned back in the hard extra chair. Why wasn't the furniture more comfortable? Made no sense to him.

"Yeah, we'll miss her."

"Go by and see her later, would you do that for me? Just check and make sure she's okay."

He leaned forward and saw Doris smile a knowing little smile. "What is it, Doris?"

"She got a call about her birth mother living not far from here, in Missouri."

"So she's going alone?"

Doris bit down on her bottom lip. "I'm pretty sure she wouldn't want me to tell everything."

He grinned at that. "Doris, I love how you suddenly decide not to say anything. I should probably go."

"Yes, you should."

He hugged her goodbye and minutes later he was

pulling up to the house at Cooper Creek. He had argued with himself all the way back to the ranch. He'd told himself that if Harmony wanted him to go with her, she would have asked. Then he told himself that Harmony didn't know what she wanted. Then again, he didn't know what he wanted, either. He knew without a doubt that she shouldn't go through something like that alone. He got that she was trying to put distance between them for the sake of the kids, but there were times that a person just needed a friend.

When he walked through the front door, Cash tackled him. He was wearing a cowboy hat, chaps and boots. And no pants.

"Where are your clothes?"

The little boy giggled and ran off in just his little-boy underwear. Dylan shook his head and walked into the living room where his mom was sitting in her favorite chair reading a book to Callie. It was a sweet sight.

"You're back earlier than I expected." His mom looked over the top of her reading glasses as he approached.

"Yeah, well, I need some information and figured you could get it for me."

"What's that?" She put the book down on her lap. Callie gave him a narrow-eyed look that led him to believe he'd interrupted a pretty good story.

"Pow, pow." A toy shotgun poked him in the back of the leg. Cash laughed and ran off.

"Buddy boy, I'm going to have to do something with you."

"Yes, like put him in a time-out once in a while, Dylan. He's becoming quite a handful."

"Yeah, I know. Mom, I need some information."

"Okay, what do you need?" She slid Callie off her

lap. He smiled as Callie wrapped strong arms around him, giving him a hug. His mom had brushed her hair and pulled it into pigtails. Unlike Cash, she was dressed in jeans and a long-sleeved T-shirt. She had a smudge of chocolate on her chin.

"I need to find out where Harmony is heading."

"Ask Harmony," his mom said with a sweet smile.

"She isn't going to tell me. And she's too stubborn to ask a friend to go with her."

"Why don't you tell me what's going on and then I'll see if I can help."

He sat on the sofa. Cash climbed up on his lap. Dylan cringed, lifting the little boy off his lap. "He's wet."

"We're potty training, Dylan. That's why he's dressed like that."

"I'll get him some clean clothes. Where's his bag?"

His mom pointed to the bag on the hall tree near the front door. "Have at it. I'm just glad he saved it for you. Also, I think there's a puddle."

Dylan headed for the kitchen to get paper towels and cleaner. He held Cash under his arm and the little boy made airplane noises. Dylan laughed. Kids.

After the floor and Cash were cleaned up, he headed back to the sofa. "Mom, I need to find out where Harmony is heading. She's going to see her birth mother. That isn't something she should face alone."

"I'll call Olivia Cross, but you need to realize she might not want anyone there."

"I'll take that into consideration," he agreed.

"Good, because I know you, and you're thinking you need to charge to the rescue." She shot a pointed look in the direction of Cash and Callie, who were playing on the floor.

She had a good point. He did have a tendency to take over. To rescue. And Harmony obviously didn't want or need to be rescued.

"This isn't about rescuing," he finally said, his mom's brows arched in disbelief. "I want to be with this woman. I want to help her get through this."

This situation wasn't the same as Katrina, or Cash and Callie. He might have started out rescuing Harmony Cross, but now he realized she'd become the person he wanted to spend time with. A lot of time.

He also knew that if he showed up in Missouri, she would think he was charging to the rescue.

Common sense told him to stay home and let her face this on her own. It wouldn't be the first time he'd ignored common sense.

"You're going, aren't you?" his mom asked.

He nodded and stood, "Yeah, I'm going."

He had a feeling she wouldn't thank him for it.

Chapter Fifteen

Harmony knocked on the door of the single-wide trailer on a parcel of land a short distance from Joplin, Missouri. The place was old and rundown. The porch had missing boards and steps that leaned. No one answered the first knock. She knocked again. Her heart hammering fast and hard. Her stomach clenching as she waited, replaying for the millionth time what it would be like to see Patricia Duncan again.

It had been twenty-three years. What would her mother look like? Would she be angry? Would she tell Harmony to leave and not come back? Her palms began to sweat. She knocked again and waited. Inside a dog barked and someone told it to be quiet.

The door flew opened and a woman looked her up and down, then glanced past her to the car in the driveway. This was the woman who had given birth to her, this woman who looked enough like Olivia Cross that a person could tell they were related. But unlike Olivia, this woman was worn. Her skin was sallow. Her blond hair had grayed. Curly blond hair. Harmony's hair. Dark blue eyes. Harmony's eyes.

"I'm not buying whatever you're selling," Patricia Duncan growled with a smoker's raspy voice.

"I'm not selling anything. I'm here to see Patricia Duncan."

"I'm her. What do you want?"

"Can I come in?" Harmony's leg shook, partly from pain, but mostly from nerves.

"I'm not about to let a stranger in my house."

"I'm not a stranger," Harmony said through the glass door that separated them.

Patricia Duncan gave Harmony a long look. Then she shook her head. "You don't look like anyone I know."

"Yes, I do." Harmony saw it in the other woman's eyes, the recognition and maybe fear.

"No, I can't say that I know you."

Harmony reached for the door handle. She was surprised that the other woman backed away and let her open it. A dog, a tiny dust mop of white fur, came out of nowhere. It barked until Harmony picked it up. It licked her face.

"Well, she doesn't usually like anyone."

"I'm not just anyone and you know that."

She had to face this woman. She needed this closure, this moment to face her past and to settle her future. Harmony knew that from this moment forward, her life would be forever changed.

Patricia pointed to the plaid upholstered sofa where a big gray cat glared at her with bright green eyes. Harmony sat on the edge and waited for her mother to sit on a wood-framed chair that matched.

"I guess I didn't expect you to find me." Her mother finally spoke, lighting a cigarette and blowing smoke up in the air. "Looks like you turned out okay. I heard about the wreck."

Her mother knew about her life. She wondered how this person could pretend to know her and yet she'd never called, never sent a letter.

"Yes, I had a wreck."

"It was a shame about your friend. It wasn't your fault, you know. I read the gossip papers and they were pretty hard on you."

It wasn't her fault. She'd been told the same in counseling, in rehab and even in group meetings at Back Street Community Center. It had been a tragic accident. A truck had run a stop sign. Amy had been the casualty. But if Harmony hadn't called her, she would still be alive.

Last week in group someone had asked how she knew that. It had made her angry to hear such a callous statement. She still didn't want to think it through. She would save that one for a rainy day in the distant future.

"Well, why are you here?" Patricia puffed on the cigarette and leaned back in the chair.

"You're my mother."

"Honey, that's where you're wrong. I'm no one's mother. I'm a woman who gave birth and abandoned her child. My sister is a mother. I knew she'd love you and she did a real good job. I'm not a bad person, I'm just not a mom. I'm barely able to take care of myself."

Harmony felt the sharp edges of anger rise to the surface. Anger at this woman.

"You left me alone in a parking lot. You could have called my mom. You could have taken me somewhere safe. You left me, not caring what happened to me."

"I…" She shook her head. "I know. Drugs do that to a person. I guess you understand that now."

"Do *not* compare me to yourself."

Patricia laughed. With bloodshot eyes and hands that shook, she laughed. Harmony knew the telltale signs of an addict: jerky arms and legs, those nervous, darting eyes, the way she tapped her foot.

"You're not me?" Patricia shook her head. "But you are. And here's a news flash, kiddo. I almost ended your life before it began. Almost. But then I couldn't do it."

The room spun, and Harmony hugged herself and stared at the woman sitting close enough to touch. She wanted to run. She wanted to fight. She shook her head and refocused on her mother. On a woman clearly in need of a fix.

Patricia Duncan must have seen the look.

She moved again, scratching sores on her arms. "I'm not clean. I'll never be clean. They say I probably won't live another year."

"Why?"

"Hepatitis. I should have got help years ago, but I didn't do the program. Didn't want to. I wanted to forget everything. Wanted to forget you."

Harmony knew how it felt to want to forget. But she now knew the danger in that. Because a person had to face their pain, their mistakes. She shook her head as the realization hit.

"I'm not you."

"No, I guess you're not. You were the lucky one. You got help and you're clean. And you're real pretty."

"What can I do to help you?"

Patricia reached to put out her cigarette. "Not much

you can do. Go live your life and be happy. That's what I always wanted for you. That's why I disappeared."

"I could get you help."

She gave Harmony a long look before shaking her head. "I have friends here that I won't leave, friends that don't judge me. You would judge me. And besides, you've been through enough."

Harmony watched as her mother began to scratch at her neck and face. "Please."

Patricia stood up and walked to the door. "No, you should go now. You need to leave. You need to understand the difference between us. I never wanted to be clean. There was no rock bottom for me. So go, now."

Because she needed a fix. Harmony knew how it worked, she knew the look. If she stayed she might delay it for thirty minutes, maybe an hour. But Patricia Duncan was a lifelong addict who didn't want to stop using.

And wanting to stop meant everything.

Patricia turned from the window. "Do you know that cowboy standing out in my yard? He looks like he's waiting for someone."

Harmony walked to the window and stood next to her mother, the closest they'd been in twenty-three years. She felt compassion, maybe love, but she knew this woman didn't belong in the role of mother. That position belonged to Olivia Cross.

She wasn't surprised to see Dylan standing next to his new truck. He nodded and raised his hat, but he didn't walk toward the trailer. He waited.

"That's one good-looking cowboy," Patricia whistled. "Are you going to marry him?"

"No, we're just friends."

Patricia turned to look at her and she smiled. "I don't need an invitation to the wedding, but I'd appreciate pictures from time to time."

She walked back across the width of the room and reached into the table next to her chair. Harmony watched as she pulled out a box and lifted the lid.

"This is my scrapbook."

Harmony saw her name across the top. She looked inside the box of mementos. There were birth pictures of her, then there were photos cut out of magazines.

Emotions welled up that took her by surprise, but she managed to nod. "There won't be a wedding, but I will send pictures. Hopefully you won't see me in any more magazines."

Patricia patted her arm. "I hope not, too. But it's been real nice talking to you and I hope you'll tell my sister that I think she did a fine job with you."

Harmony hugged her mother, holding tight for a minute, until Patricia pulled back. She cleared her throat and looked away from Harmony. After a minute she reached down and grabbed the white fluff of a dog.

"Will you take him?" She handed the dog to Harmony. "I don't know what's going to happen to me in the next year. I have a friend who'll take the cat. But I'd like for you to have the dog. I don't have anything else to give you."

"You don't have to," Harmony wanted to say, but instead she took the dog that was shoved into her hands.

"Go now. I guess you know you have to go."

Harmony nodded, and with tears blurring her vision, she made it down the steps and across the yard. She stumbled and strong hands reached out, grabbing her, pulling her close. Big hands smoothed her hair and a familiar voice told her it would be okay.

"Don't you ever listen?" she finally blubbered into his shoulder, the material soaked from her tears.

"Never." He brushed a hand through her hair.

"You didn't have to do this."

"Yes, I did. And if you hadn't been so stubborn I could have driven you up here." He pulled back a foot. "Did you know you're holding a fluffy white rat?"

"It's my dog." She sobbed into the fluffy fur. "She gave me a dog."

"You should have told me, Harmony. You didn't have to do this alone."

"Yes, I did. I came here to face the truth of who I am and I didn't want you to see."

"I am looking at the person you are. The person who takes a rat dog and hugs a lady that abandoned her."

"I'm also the person who hated her and had to work hard to forgive her." She looked up into hazel eyes that melted her resolve. "I didn't want to take you on this trip with me."

There, she'd said it. He'd been through enough. She couldn't let him go through all of this with her. But she could see from the look in his eyes that he wasn't going to let her off the hook so easily.

"You're in no condition to drive," he said, reaching for her hands as they trembled. She tried to pull free but he didn't let go. He wouldn't let her go. Not without fighting for what he knew they could have together.

"Dylan, I'm fine. I promise, I'm completely sober."

"That isn't what I mean and you know it." He led her

to her car. "You're still shaking. Let's go get some coffee. I think I saw a diner a mile or so back."

"I saw it, too."

"I'll follow you." He opened her car door and when she was behind the wheel with the dog on her lap, he closed it.

He didn't know what to say to her when they got to the café. He didn't know how to tell her he'd been worried about her. Worried that her mother would break her heart again. He didn't want her to go through that. But what could he say, when it was obvious she planned to leave soon.

They took a seat in a far booth of the bare-bones little diner. The booths were orange vinyl, the tables black Formica. A waitress walked out of the back looking surprised to have customers.

"Two coffees, please," Dylan ordered then looked at Harmony. "Are you hungry?"

"Pie would be nice."

"We have cake." The waitress looked at her. "Do you want cake?"

Harmony nodded, her eyes wide. When the waitress walked away, she looked at him, grinning. "She isn't Vera."

"No, she isn't," he agreed.

"So, do you want to know?"

He shrugged. "What do you want to tell me?"

She told him everything, spilling it all, including the continued fear of becoming Patricia Duncan. But he saw that the fear had lessened. Something had changed.

"Dylan, what if DNA is stronger than the love my parents had for me? What if I slip?"

"You're what, 170 days clean and sober? Do you think Patricia has ever gone thirty days without using?"

"I'm not sure. I just don't want to be her. I don't want to be the kind of woman who leaves a child behind."

He hadn't expected those words to hurt, but they did. "I think women don't always choose to leave their children behind, Harmony."

She looked down, her hands clasped together on the Formica table. "No, I know they don't and I'm sorry. But I can end this pattern of behavior."

"What, by staying single? By not having children?" He was angry now because she still didn't see. "Harmony…"

She looked up. "What do you want me to say?"

"I guess I want you to see the person I see. I want you to have some faith in yourself."

"I'm working on that."

"I love you." The words slipped out. He closed his eyes and wished he hadn't said them, not yet. Talk about the worst possible timing.

Her eyes widened. "You can't love me."

The waitress suddenly appeared with coffee and cake. She set it down in front of them, asked if they needed anything else and left. Harmony pushed the cake away. Yeah, he didn't have much of an appetite either.

"You can't love me."

He rubbed the back of his neck and looked at the woman sitting across from him. Man, he loved her. More than he ever could have guessed, he loved her. And like an idiot he had put it all out there. "I really don't have a choice, Harmony. It isn't something that I planned."

"No, I'm sure it's the last thing you planned."

"Thanks." He lifted the cup and took a sip of the worst coffee he'd ever had. At least the bitter taste of the coffee took his mind off the bitter taste of her rejection.

"I'm the last thing you need, Dylan. You need someone without all of this baggage. Cash and Callie need someone…"

"Who loves them the way you love them. Not every woman is going to want a single cowboy with two little kids to raise, Harmony. Not every woman is going to love those two kids."

"Dylan, please…" She flicked away a tear that had rolled down her cheek, then reached for a napkin to wipe away more tears. "I'm the last person you need in your life."

"You are the only person I want in my life, Harmony."

"I wish you hadn't done this."

"I'm glad I did. I want you to think about it, about the four of us together."

"That's exactly what I'm trying to tell you. This isn't just about you and me."

"I know it isn't." He reached for her hand. "And I also know this is about you being afraid of losing someone again. You think you're easy to walk away from…"

She shook her head. "Don't."

"I'm going to say this, Harmony. I'm going to tell you that you're the last person I would walk away from."

"If I fall…"

"I'd pick you back up."

"You want to spend your life that way? Do you want to always wonder if I'm hiding something, or worry that I'm using?"

"I'd pick you up every single day, if I had to."

She smiled at that and he felt relieved for a minute.

"That's sweet, but you know it isn't that easy. You haven't had to live with addiction. You've only dealt with the aftermath, not the stuff that tears a person apart."

"No, I haven't."

She pushed her coffee aside and scooted out of the booth. She smiled down at him. He had a bad feeling growing inside him.

"I can't let you do that to yourself, Dylan. I don't want you trying to fix me."

"Do you realize how much you've been picking *me* up, Harmony? How much you've fixed *my* life?"

"It's easy to help you." She grabbed her purse and leaned to kiss his cheek. "That's what we've been doing, helping each other."

"Harmony, you know it's more than that. Somewhere along the way, it became much more."

She shook her head. "I've loved helping you with the kids. I've loved…"

"What? You've loved what?" He wanted her to say the words, that she loved him.

"We have to stop now. We both have to go back to our lives."

She walked out the door. Dylan thought about letting her go but couldn't. He tossed a ten on the table, and followed Harmony out to her car.

"Do you love me?"

She got behind the wheel and looked up at him.

"Dylan, I hurt the people I love. It's what I've always done. I don't want to hurt you, too."

Too late.

He watched her drive away, then he walked back to his truck knowing he'd blown it. He hadn't told a woman he loved her since high school. And that definitely hadn't been love. That had been a Friday night with a pretty cowgirl and no thought of forever. At the time he'd been pretty confused about what love meant.

Now he knew exactly what love was, and how it felt to want to hold a woman forever. Now if he could just convince her to trust herself—and him—enough to be loved.

Chapter Sixteen

On Friday, Harmony walked through the Cross farm-house one last time. Her suitcase was already in the car. This was goodbye, to this house, to Dawson, to the life she had lived here. She stopped in the kitchen to look out at the pasture. Blake Cooper was driving a farm truck and cattle were following behind him. No doubt he'd probably buy the place if her dad put it up for sale.

Her heart broke a little thinking that it wouldn't belong to her family much longer.

It had been her refuge these last weeks. It had been the place where she'd put herself back together. She wiped at the tears burning her eyes and told herself to stop crying. She had to get on with life.

She had to get back to her life before the alcohol, before the accident and pills. She knew that she was more than the person she'd become over the last few years. She was better than this, than the person who hid behind a high, or used a high to fake happiness.

God had not created her to fail. She took a deep breath and reminded herself of the message she'd heard from Dawson Community Church the previous week. God had created her with a purpose.

She picked up the dog Patricia had given her. Its tag said Whizz, so that's what she called it. She thought it probably wasn't the best name but the puppy answered to it.

In twenty-six years, Patricia Duncan had given her daughter three precious gifts. Life. A family. And a puppy.

It mattered.

She made one last loop, making sure all of the lights were off, then she walked out the door. She didn't look back. On her way out of town she planned to say good-bye to Doris and Bill.

She needed to remind Bill to feed Beau until she could arrange for someone to haul the horse to Nashville. Her horse. She knew he wasn't worth much, but in a way, the horse had saved her life. He had given her something to focus on, a distraction.

When she pulled up to the Tanner's house, she saw them both sitting on the front porch. Doris was home for the weekend. If everything went the way they wanted, she'd be home for good in a few days.

Harmony carried the puppy up the sidewalk and she remembered back to the first time she'd pulled up this driveway. She stopped in front of Bill and smiled at the man who had become an unexpected friend.

"I'm leaving."

Bill shook his head and looked at Doris. She answered for them both. "We wish you wouldn't."

"It's time for me to go home."

Doris's lips thinned. "I think you're running, but that's between you and God. And Dylan Cooper."

"I'm not…"

She couldn't lie.

Doris smiled at her.

"Okay, maybe I am running. But this is for the best. For Dylan. For the kids. It'll hurt less if I leave now than if I let them down later."

"Why are you so sure you'll let people down?" Bill spoke, his voice shaking a little and his hand clenched. "I've never met a young woman so determined to think she can't do right."

"I'm… I'm just…"

"Determined." He pointed a finger at her. "Be determined to make the right choices, not determined to mess up."

"I'm…" She didn't know what else to say. "You'll feed Beau for me and take him treats?"

"Told you I would."

Harmony handed Doris a gift bag and watched as the older woman opened it. She pulled the pale blue shawl out of the tissue paper.

"I made it myself. I think I finally figured out how to count stitches."

Doris wrapped the gift around her shoulders. "I think you were determined to get it right."

"Yes, I guess I was."

Doris reached for her hand and pulled her close. "Harmony, let yourself be loved. Take a chance. I did, fifty years ago. And look how it worked out for me. This old man, I couldn't imagine my life without him. And I almost walked away. Almost went to California to live with a cousin. I'm so glad I stayed and gave it a chance."

"Doris, I don't know what I'd do without you. I'm going to miss you. But I'm not you. This isn't the same."

"Oh, it isn't so different. But you go and remember you have a home and people who love you here. I'm going to miss you, Harmony Cross. I'll miss you a lot. But I'm not going to miss you near as much as Dylan and those two kids will."

Harmony choked back a sob. "I have to go."

"No, you just think you have to. Now give me a hug and you do me a favor."

"What's that?"

"First, remember to visit. Second, pray about this. You're headstrong and determined, but that doesn't always mean you're right."

She nodded, hugged Doris, then Bill, and finally she left. As she drove out of town she looked in her rearview mirror thinking, hoping, that maybe Dylan would come after her. She kept her promise to Doris; she prayed. As she prayed, she thought of a million things that she should have taken care of.

What if Dylan forgot where she'd ordered Cash's cake? Who would fix Callie's hair for the party?

As she drove toward Arkansas, she thought about texting Heather or Eva to make sure someone knew where to find that cake. She thought about being the person who didn't let everyone down. Including herself.

Walking away was easier than staying. If she didn't commit herself, she didn't have to feel guilty if she messed up.

Just like Patricia Duncan.

The thought left her unsettled. Even as she drove, she knew she couldn't be that person, the one who walked away. She'd learned a lot about herself in Dawson, and in the end, wasn't that why she'd come home? Because she'd known in Dawson she would find herself. She would find her faith.

She would find her heart.

Chapter Seventeen

Dylan didn't know why he drove by the Cross Ranch on his way to town, but he did. He guessed he hoped Harmony would be there, that she might have changed her mind. But she was gone. Her car wasn't in the garage. The lights were all turned off and the doors were locked.

Beau whinnied from the pasture. She had promised to find someone to haul the horse to Nashville. He thought he might load the animal up and drive him down there some time. After giving the animal an extra can of grain, he got in his truck and headed to town.

It was Cash's birthday and Dylan had other things to do besides worrying about Harmony leaving town. He glanced at the address written on paper left in the console of his truck. It had the name, address and phone number of the baker who was making the train-shaped cake Harmony had ordered.

He guessed a cake she picked was better than nothing. But Cash and Callie weren't as easily convinced. They wanted her back. He did, too.

Cash and Callie were with Heather. She was fixing

Callie's hair and getting Cash dressed in new clothes. He was turning two. It was an important birthday. And it was hard, having birthdays without Katrina. It mattered more to Callie. She remembered how it should have felt. Callie's third birthday had been a big deal with pizza and a trip to the circus, because they'd known they needed to make it special.

He pulled up to the bakery, and went inside as a young woman walked out from the back. "Can I help you?"

"I'm here to pick up a birthday cake."

She looked surprised. "Did you order one?"

Oh, great, just what he didn't need. "Yes, I did."

"There must be a mistake. We had one birthday cake but the customer picked it up an hour ago."

"This can't be happening. Today is my son's second birthday. We, I mean, my friend ordered a train cake for Cash Cooper."

Her mouth formed an *O*. "You mean Harmony Cross?"

"Yes." He wanted to close his eyes and count to ten but he didn't. He waited, hoping the light was coming on here.

"She picked the cake up an hour ago."

"She picked the cake up? Are you sure it was her? She left town."

"Oh, yes, I'm sure I know who Harmony is."

"You're positive?"

"Yes, I am. She said she was afraid you wouldn't remember where she bought it and she didn't want that little guy to be let down on his birthday. She was real sweet about it. She even ordered a special pink cupcake for your daughter."

He tipped his hat and walked out the door to his

truck, stuck somewhere between madder than an old hornet and happier than a kitten with a bowl of cream.

He didn't call her. Instead he headed for the ranch. But first he stopped at his grandmother's house. She and Winston were getting ready for the party.

"Dylan, what in the world are you doing here."

He kissed his grandmother's cheek. "I left something here."

"You left something here?" And then her eyes lit up. "Why, yes, you did. I had forgotten all about that. Let me go see if I can find it. You have a better memory than I do."

"There are some things a guy can't forget, Gran."

"Well, isn't that the truth. Winston is forgetful but he never forgets where he left me."

She chuckled as she walked away, leaving him waiting in the entry of her big Victorian house. Winston came out of the kitchen, gave him a look, one that said he couldn't remember which Cooper was standing in his house. In his defense, there were more than a few of them.

"Dylan," Dylan reminded his stepgrandfather.

"Of course, Dylan. Where's your young 'uns?"

"With my sister Heather."

"Well, that's just fine. I guess we'll see you at the ranch for the party?"

"Yes, we will." Granny Myrna came down the steps and handed him a box. "I think this is going to be quite the party."

"Gran, I love you. You're the soul of discretion."

She smiled. "Yes, I am."

He pulled up to the ranch a few minutes later, more nervous than he'd ever been in his life. What if Harmony wasn't there? He brushed a hand across his face. He saw her car on the other side of Lucky's SUV. Dylan hopped out of his truck, wiping his sweaty palms on his jeans.

Then she was there, coming down the steps of his parents' house. She looked beautiful, like a fall afternoon. She wore a long, dark blue sweater and jeans tucked into riding boots. Her blond hair was loose and the breeze caught it, lifting it.

"Surprise," she said as he walked up to her.

She was everything he wanted, and more. He hoped that she felt the same about him.

Harmony didn't know what to do. She stood on the last step, holding the rail, waiting for him to react, to say something. She'd planned this moment. She'd stopped at a hotel in a little town in Arkansas and realized that she was strong, she was a survivor.

She had also realized that she couldn't handle the idea of going back to Tennessee, not with three people she loved left behind in Oklahoma. She had called her parents and explained that she might be delayed.

"How long are you here for?" Dylan finally asked, pulling off the cowboy hat and running fingers through flattened hair. She wanted to touch his hair, remembering that it was soft beneath her fingers with just the slightest curl.

"I think a while." She swallowed the fear and found determination. "I asked my dad to keep the ranch. I might want to live there."

"Really?" His brows arched and she saw a hint of a smile.

"Yes, really. It's my home, you know. Nowhere else has ever felt the way this place feels."

"I'm glad to hear that. We missed you." She nodded and took the last step, thankful for the hand on her arm. His hand.

"Dylan, I need to be honest."

He grinned now. "Because it's required?"

"No, well, yes. But I need to be honest because if I'm not, I'm going to fall apart. My heart isn't going to be whole. I'll…"

He stopped her words with the sweetest kiss. His hands held hers and he held her close. He kissed her twice, the second time whispering her name against her lips before holding her captive in the sweetest possible way. She leaned close, needing more of him.

When he pulled back she looked up, into the hazel eyes of a cowboy who made her understand, without a doubt, that something was meant to be.

"I came back to tell you I love you, Dylan." She brushed a hand across his cheek. "I love that you're kind and generous. I love your faith. I love that you love Cash and Callie."

"I love you." He kissed her again. "Oh, Harmony, I love you and I can't lose you."

"You're not losing me."

"Good, because I was thinking that I would have to deliver Beau to Nashville. Anything for another chance to convince you that we need you here with us."

Suddenly Cash and Callie zoomed down the steps and grabbed her, two pairs of arms tight around her legs. Dylan held her steady and she smiled up at him, falling in love all over again.

"Kids, get back in here." Angie Cooper walked out

the front door, wiping her hands on her apron. "I'm sorry. I couldn't stop them."

"They can stay." Dylan reached into his pocket. "This concerns them, too."

"Dylan." Shivers ran up Harmony's arms.

"I've loved you forever, Harmony, so this doesn't feel like rushing into something for me. It feels like now is the perfect time."

She started to answer but he kissed her.

"That seems like the best way to keep you quiet." He whispered near her ear after kissing her into stunned silence.

"I can't let you walk away. I can't promise things will always be easy. But I can promise to always pick you up when you fall."

"I'll pick you up, too." She swayed a little as Cash and Callie circled her, jumping up and down.

Dylan grabbed both kids, one under each arm. They grinned big.

"Marry us, Harmony Cross." He put Callie on the ground and held out a ring with a beautiful pink stone surrounded by diamonds. "Marry me."

"I think I will."

He slipped the ring on her finger and then kissed her again, but Cash grabbed her neck, throwing her off balance. The four of them fell to the ground in a laughing heap. Yes, this was exactly what Harmony Cross needed.

She needed this family. She needed this man and these kids.

Forever.

Epilogue

Because they had only dated weeks when Dylan proposed, they decided on a long engagement, marrying in the spring. Harmony wanted this marriage more than anything.

And inside her wedding shoe was something new, a coin proclaiming 335 days clean and sober. Because she was determined to succeed. She had three very good reasons, three people she couldn't let down.

As they stood in the fellowship hall of the Dawson Community Church waiting for the ceremony to begin, she smiled at this family that had become hers. And the family she already had that loved her.

Lila was her maid of honor, of course. Lila with her beautiful smile, a smile she'd been using on Bryan Cooper for the last week. Bryan, who'd finally come home from South America, to his mother's delight.

Heather was a bridesmaid, along with Sophie, Eva and Mia.

Sometimes Harmony had a moment that took her by surprise, when sadness crept up on her. She thought of

Amy, and how Amy would have been there, in a pale pink dress, her blond hair framing her face.

But a little bit of Amy was with Harmony. She wore a necklace her friend had given her years ago. A cheap BFF necklace. Best Friends Forever.

But Harmony knew her friend would have been happy to witness this moment, to see her friend clean and sober, to see her happy.

It was a bittersweet thought.

She blinked away tears as her mom came through the door, a smiling woman with blond hair and blue eyes filling with tears.

"This is a no-cry zone," Heather warned with a shake of her finger.

"I can't help it," Olivia Cross sniffled. "I wish my sister was here to see."

"She wouldn't come. But I'll send her pictures."

"It's almost time." Olivia hugged her tight. "I love you."

"I love you, too. And thank you for not giving up on me."

"You're my daughter. I couldn't give up."

Then it was time. They walked down the hallway to the front of the church. The bridesmaids went first. Harmony stood waiting, her hand on her dad's arm.

"I love you, Daddy."

He cleared his throat. "I love you, too. This is what you want, right?"

"It's what I've wanted all my life."

"I have a gift for you. That little place down the road. It's your ranch now. Yours and Dylan's."

"Thank you so much," she whispered, tears rolling

down her cheeks. Her dad pushed a handkerchief in her hand and she dabbed her eyes.

"I'm going to be the bride that got married with raccoon eyes."

"You'll be the prettiest bride ever," her dad whispered back.

"You have to say that, you're my daddy."

"Yes, I am."

The music started and they began their trip down the aisle. She smiled at Dylan. He had turned to watch her, that cowboy of hers. But today he wasn't a cowboy. Today he wore a suit. He'd shaved. And just looking at him made her heart do a funny dance.

He was *her* cowboy. Her man.

As they went down the aisle, she smiled at Granny Myrna whose ring was on her left hand. Myrna had explained that this ring with the pink stone had been an anniversary gift from her husband, Milt. That made it even more special. Cash and Callie were at the front of the church, the ring bearer and flower girl.

There were several flower girls, actually. Callie was joined by Jackson's newest daughter, just adopted six months ago from Texas. Next to her was Keeton and Sophie's daughter, Lucy. She was just barely three and she knew how to wrap everyone around her little finger.

Harmony's dad handed her over to Dylan with warning look. "Take care of my girl."

People around them laughed. Dylan smiled at her and her knees went a little weak. He reached for her hand even though Wyatt Johnson had told them to wait until he gave the command to take her hand. Dylan ignored him.

They repeated their vows, holding hands and waiting for that special moment at the end, the moment they had been waiting for now for seven months.

"I now pronounce you husband and wife," Wyatt said. And then he didn't say more. Dylan shot him a look and Wyatt laughed.

"You may kiss the bride."

He gathered her up, crushing her beautiful dress in the process, but she didn't care. She cared about this man. She cared that when he held her, she felt stronger.

"I love you, Harmony Cooper."

"I love you, too, Dylan Cooper."

They hurried down the aisle with bubbles blowing around them. As they stepped outside, fireworks blasted through the night sky.

It was a very happy ending.

* * * * *

Dear Reader,

I hope you enjoy *Single Dad Cowboy,* Dylan Cooper's story. This is the last of the Cooper Creek books and it wasn't easy for me to say goodbye. The wonderful thing is that through books, we can continue to visit Dawson and the Coopers. We'll never have to leave the Mad Cow Café. We'll always be able to take a moment with Granny Myrna Cooper.

Dylan's heroine is Harmony Cross. She is facing a struggle that real people face every single day. Addiction can strike anyone. It doesn't choose between the educated, uneducated, poor, wealthy, teens or homeless. Addiction strikes moms, dads, pastors, children, grandparents—the list goes on. It takes strength and courage to face addiction and to fight the battle to overcome.

Brenda Minton

Questions for Discussion

1. *Single Dad Cowboy* begins with Harmony Cross trying to buy a horse that isn't worth much to anyone but her. Why does she want this horse?

2. Harmony Cross wants a place to be alone. Why is space important to her?

3. Dylan Cooper isn't looking for romance, although everyone in town thinks he needs a woman. Why would having a woman in his life make a difference?

4. Does Harmony fit stereotypes? If so, which ones and why?

5. What does Harmony expect to find in Dawson?

6. Dylan's plan for himself and Harmony is a platonic relationship, helping each other. How could things go wrong with such a relationship?

7. Why is Harmony worried about letting people down?

8. We all know that we need to forgive people who hurt us. There are people who need to forgive Harmony. Why does she need to forgive herself?

9. Dylan is raising Cash and Callie, but it hasn't really hit him that they are his kids. When does this begin to happen?

10. When does Harmony begin to trust herself more?

11. What changes take place in her spiritual life that increase her chances of staying clean?

12. Why is it important for her to meet the mother who abandoned her?

13. How does the recovery program change things for Harmony? What does she learn that will help her in the future, not only with addiction?

14. It is easy to look at a family like the Coopers and expect them to be perfect. No one is perfect, though, and the Coopers have had their share of struggles. How do the struggles change them, affect their faith or their family?

15. What changes for Harmony when she realizes she can be the person who loves Dylan Cooper and his kids?

COMING NEXT MONTH FROM
Love Inspired®

Available June 17, 2014

HER MONTANA COWBOY
Big Sky Centennial • by Valerie Hansen

When rodeo cowboy Ryan Travers comes to town, mayor's daughter Julie Shaw can't keep her eyes off him. Amid Jasper Gulch's centennial celebrations, they just may find true love!

THE BACHELOR NEXT DOOR
Castle Falls • by Kathryn Springer

Successful businessman Brendan Kane has made little room in his life for fun. Will his mother's hiring of Lily Michaels to renovate his family home bring him the laughter—and love—he's been missing?

REDEEMING THE RANCHER
Serendipity Sweethearts • by Deb Kastner

City boy Griff Haddon never thought he'd fall for the small town community of Serendipity—especially beautiful rancher Alexis Grainger. If he can forget his past hurts, this may just be his second chance at forever.

SMALL-TOWN HOMECOMING
Moonlight Cove • by Lissa Manley

Musician Curt Graham returns to Moonlight Cove to start a new life. Can beautiful innkeeper Jenna Flaherty see beyond his bad boy past and build a future together?

FOREVER A FAMILY
Rosewood, Texas • by Bonnie K. Winn

Widow Olivia Gray hopes volunteering at Rosewood's veterinary clinic will help her troubled son. But is veterinarian Zeke Harrison also the key to healing her broken heart?

THEIR UNEXPECTED LOVE
Second Time Around • by Kathleen Y'Barbo

Working together on a ministry project, Logan Burkett and spirited Pipa Gallagher clash from the beginning. Will they ever move past their differences and see that sometimes opposites really *do* attract?

LICNM0614

REQUEST YOUR FREE BOOKS!

2 FREE INSPIRATIONAL NOVELS

PLUS 2 FREE MYSTERY GIFTS

Love Inspired

SPECIAL EXCERPT FROM

Love Inspired

*Join the ranching town of Jasper Gulch, Montana,
as they celebrate 100 years!*

Here's a sneak peek at
HER MONTANA COWBOY
by Valerie Hansen, the first of six books in the
BIG SKY CENTENNIAL *miniseries.*

For the first time in longer than Ryan Travers could re-call, he was having trouble keeping his mind on his work. He couldn't have cared less about Jasper Gulch's missing time capsule; it was pretty Julie Shaw who occupied his thoughts.

"That's not good," he muttered as he stood on a metal rung of the narrow bucking chute. This rangy pinto mare wasn't called Widow-maker for nothing. He could not only picture Julie Shaw as if she were standing right there next to the chute gates, he could imagine her light, uplifting laughter.

Actually, he realized with a start, that *was* what he was hearing. He started to glance over his shoulder, intending to scan the nearby crowd and, hopefully, locate her.

"Clock's ticking, Travers," the chute boss grumbled. "You gonna ride that horse or just look at her?"

Rather than answer with words, Ryan stepped across the top of the chute, raised his free hand over his head and leaned way back. Then he nodded to the gateman.

The latch clicked.

The mare leaped.

Ryan didn't attempt to do anything but ride until he heard the horn blast announcing his success. Then he straightened as best he could and worked his fingers loose with his free hand while pickup men maneuvered close enough to help him dismount.

To Ryan's delight, Julie Shaw and a few others he recognized from before were watching. They had parked a flatbed farm truck near the fence beside the grandstand and were watching from secure perches in its bed.

Julie had both arms raised and was still cheering so wildly she almost knocked her hat off. "Woo-hoo! Good ride, cowboy!"

Ryan's "Thanks" was swallowed up in the overall din from the rodeo fans. Clearly, Julie wasn't the only spectator who had been favorably impressed.

He knew he should immediately report to the area behind the strip chutes and pick up his rigging. And he would. In a few minutes. As soon as he'd spoken to his newest fan.

Don't miss the romance between Julie and rodeo hero Ryan in HER MONTANA COWBOY by Valerie Hansen, available July 2014 from Love Inspired®.

SPECIAL EXCERPT FROM

When a widow is stalked and taunted by memories from her tragic past, can the man who rescued her years ago come to her aid again?

Read on for a preview of PROTECTIVE INSTINCTS by Shirlee McCoy, the first book in her brand-new **MISSION: RESCUE** *series.*

"Who would want to hurt you, Raina?" Jackson asked her.

"No one," she replied, her mind working frantically, going through faces and names and situations.

"And yet, someone chased you through the woods. That same person nearly ran me down. Doesn't sound like someone who feels all warm and fuzzy when he thinks of you."

"Maybe he was a vagrant, and I scared him."

"Maybe." He didn't sound like he believed it, and she wasn't sure she did, either.

She'd heard something that had woken her from the nightmare.

A child crying? Her neighbor Larry wandering around? An intruder trying to get into the house?

The last thought made her shudder, and she pulled her coat a little closer. "I think I'd know it if someone had a bone to pick with me."

"That's usually the case, but not always. Could be you upset a coworker, said no to a guy who wanted you to say yes—"

She snorted at that, and Jackson frowned. "You've been a widow for four years. It's not that far-fetched an idea."

"If you got a good look at my social life you wouldn't be saying that."

Samuel yawned loudly and slid down on the pew, his arms crossed over his chest, his eyelids drooping. The ten-year-old looked cold and tired, and she wanted to get him home and tuck him into bed.

"I'll go talk to Officer Wallace," Jackson responded. "See if he's ready to let us leave."

"He's going to have to be. Samuel—"

A door slammed, the sound so startling Raina jumped.

She grabbed Samuel's shoulder, pulled him into the shelter of her arms.

"Is someone else in the church?" Jackson demanded, his gaze on the door that led from the sanctuary into the office wing.

"There shouldn't be."

"Stay put. I'm going to check things out."

He strode away, and she wanted to call out and tell him to be careful.

She pressed her lips together, held in the words she knew she didn't need to say. She'd seen him in action, knew just how smart and careful he was.

Jackson could take care of himself.

*Will Jackson discover the stalker and help
Raina find a second chance at love?*

*Pick up PROTECTIVE INSTINCTS to find out.
Available July 2014 wherever
Love Inspired® Suspense books are sold.*

Love Inspired

THE BACHELOR NEXT DOOR

by

Kathryn Springer

Dedicating all his time to the family business isn't easy for Brendan Kane. But he owes his foster parents big-time for taking him and his brothers in. And if he has to give up the possibility of a relationship—so be it. So when Brendan's mother hires Lily Michaels to redecorate the family home, it doesn't matter to Brendan that Lily is beautiful. And funny. And smart. He has no time for distractions. Can Lily show him there's more to life…and that it includes a future together?

Castle Falls

Three rugged brothers meet their matches.

Available July 2014 wherever
Love Inspired books and ebooks are sold.

Find us on Facebook at
www.Facebook.com/LoveInspiredBooks

LI87896